USED BITCOIN

by Robert Rahula

ALSO BY ROBERT RAHULA

NOVELS:
Messieurs
Panamaniac
Island of Misfits
Day Another Paradise In
One Last Fling
Bathhouse Stories
Conversation in a Belgian Bar
All the Yage in Reno
Exigent Circumstances
Uninvited Guest
A Modest Summation of Things
To Die in Toledo
The Treasure of the Gran Ventura
Inauthenticity
Weightless
The Erikschitz Principle
The Dopa Project

SHORT STORIES:
Horror Stories for Children
Behind the Pearly Gates

POETRY:
Trigger Points
Dentro Del Corazón Bloqueada
Camino
Migration
I Sing the Body Politic
Wonderland
From Whose Bourn
Poemas Españoles
Expat Poems
Old Dogs New Poems

ANTHOLOGIES:
Half Life
The Essential Dan Landes
50 Years Down the Drain

USED BITCOIN

© 2025 by Robert Rahula

All rights reserved. This book or any portion thereof may not be reproduced or used in any manner whatsoever without the express written permission of the author except for the use of brief quotations in a book review.

www.robertrahula.com

This is a work of fiction. Characters, organizations, businesses, products, locales, and events portrayed in this book either are products of the author's imagination or are used fictitiously.

Thanks to Red Dress Press, Liz, Chris, and Em for editing, proofreading, and artwork.

ISBN 979-8-9897238-4-3

Alma-gator Press
Barcelona • Madrid • La Chorrera

CHAPTER ONE

Our story begins in the tiny pueblo of Villa Rosario... Well, I really can't call it a pueblo anymore. It's grown over the years. It's no longer exactly tiny. But it's not quite large enough to call it a city. And I can't call it a villa, because that's part of its name. I couldn't say, "in the tiny villa of Villa Rosario." It doesn't sound right. So, I'll stick with pueblo, which is Spanish for town. I probably should say "pueblo viejo" which means "old town."

Our story begins in the old pueblo of Villa Rosario, which is located in the country of Panama. Villa Rosario is an old town, located about thirty minutes down the road from the city of La Chorrera... Wait, that's redundant, isn't it? I've already told you that Villa Rosario was an old town, and here I am, saying it again. Sorry. Let's start over.

Our story begins in Villa Rosario, Panama. Villa Rosario is an old town, located about thirty minutes down the road from the city of La Chorrera. And La Chorrera is located about forty-five minutes down the road from Panama City, the capital of Panama. Driving west from Panama City to Villa Rosario is like driving back through time. The decades peel off your windshield as the miles pass, until you arrive in what looks like the nineteen-fifties. You park along the dusty streets of Villa Rosario next to the old Catholic Church, and for a few minutes you sit inside your air-conditioned rental car and watch the horse-drawn carts loaded with rusted tin roofing go trudging by. On the metal gate to the church is a sign advertising an upcoming bingo game. You look at the broken sidewalks, at the barbed wire strung across the tops of all the metal fences, then higher, at the massive amounts of tangled telephone and electric lines that loop from pole to pole, and you think to yourself,

"Yup, I'm in Central America." And you dread to step out of your car, because you know it's going to be unbearably hot and humid.

Anyway, that's Villa Rosario at first glance. It doesn't leave a good impression. But underneath, it's an interesting town with an infamous history. But we'll get to that later. This story concerns one Hector Gonzalez. Hector is the fifteen-year-old nephew of one José Fernando. José Fernando—or, don Fernando, as he is known to everyone—is the police chief of Villa Rosario, and he has been the police chief for at least twenty-five, maybe thirty years, for as long as anyone can remember. He got the job when he was very young, when he killed a brujo—or witch doctor—who had been terrorizing the town by kidnapping and killing the children of the town. But that's a story for another day. The important thing here is that don Fernando is the police chief of the town, and he has a nephew named Hector Gonzalez, and Hector is fifteen.

Fifteen is a difficult age. Well, actually, every age is a difficult age. But when you're fifteen, you feel that you're at the most difficult age. And you tell yourself that if you can just hold on until you are sixteen, everything will be alright. At sixteen, you can get a driver's license in Panama, and then the world will be your oyster. Hector had never seen an oyster, but he wanted to be sixteen and he wanted the world. And if his friends told him that the world would be his oyster at sixteen, well, then, so be it.

Speaking of Hector's friends, they weren't very bright. They went to school because that's what their parents told them they had to do. But Hector was different. He liked school. Of course, he never told his friends that. There are things you just have to keep hidden if you want to have friends. But the truth was, Hector was a bright boy. And more than bright, he was ambitious. He didn't just want a driver's license, like all his friends did. Everyone at fifteen wants a driver's license, so they can beg their parents to let them drive the old family car once in a blue moon. No,

Hector wanted more than just a driver's license. He wanted a car of his very own. And for that, he needed money.

Now, you need to understand how it is for a fifteen-year-old boy in Panama who wants money. You need to see the world from his perspective. Hector looked around his world and realized that no one that he knew had money. Some people in Panama had money, but they didn't live in Villa Rosario. Hector had been to Panama City with his father once or twice. He had seen the big buildings and the men in clean suits. They were bankers, his father had explained to Hector. Bankers handled rich people's money, and for that, they charged fees. That's how bankers became rich, Hector's father explained.

"So, they make money just by handling other people's money?" Hector had asked.

His father nodded yes.

"And they don't grow any crops?" Hector asked.

His father answered, "No."

"And they don't build anything?" Hector asked.

"No," his father replied. "They just handle money."

Hector thought about this for a minute. He knew that there were people who *laundered* money in Villa Rosario. He knew a man who used to sell marijuana in the park but also owned a hamburger shop. And that man claimed that his money came from selling lots of hamburgers. But everyone knew he didn't sell lots of hamburgers because his hamburger stand was always empty. One day Hector's uncle don Fernando arrested the man, and the hamburger shop closed down and never reopened.

And so, Hector asked his father, "And what these bankers do is legal?"

"Oh, yes. Quite legal," his father had said.

"So, they don't get arrested and go to jail?" Hector asked.

"Oh, no," his father laughed.

Hector thought about this for a moment. Then he asked his father, "Can I be a banker?"

Hector's father nodded and said, "Of course. But you will have to stay in school, and then go to the university and study finance. Then, after you are twenty-one, you can get a job in a bank, and work hard. And then maybe, one day, you can be a banker."

Hector thought long and hard about this. He didn't want to wait until he was twenty-one. There must be some easier way to become a banker, he thought.

He would just have to figure it out.

CHAPTER TWO

Don Fernando. You remember him? He's the police chief of Villa Rosario, and he's also Hector Gonzalez's uncle... Well, don Fernando's best friend is Dan Landes. Now, don Fernando is 100% Panamanian. He can trace his ancestors back at least six generations. But Dan Landes is a gringo, 100% from the United States, which means he has no idea who his ancestors were. And yet, don Fernando and Dan Landes are best friends, which is a rare thing in Panama. I mean, Panamanians can have gringo "friends" in the same way that you can have work friends—you know—like people who work in the same department as you for ten years. Technically, those coworkers are your friends, but once that job ends, you never see them again. But don Fernando and Dan Landes were actual friends—best friends—and as I said, that is rare because it's hard to be a friend with a gringo; and by gringo, I mean someone from the United States. It's hard to be a friend with a gringo because gringos are so unreliable. Gringos *act* friendly; they *act* like they care about you and your culture; but most of them don't. They can't help it. It's their culture. The US raises people to only think about themselves. It's the basis for capitalism—complete and utter selfishness.

But somehow, Dan Landes was different, and he and don Fernando treated each other like brothers. And so it was that on this particular day, don Fernando called his friend Dan Landes and asked to get together for coffee, because he had a problem he wanted to discuss.

And so Dan met don Fernando at a small café called Soda Linda, and that's where Dan learned about don Fernando's nephew, Hector Gonzalez.

"Dani, I am worried about my nephew," don Fernando said.

"Oh, yeah? Which one?"

"Hector. Hector Gonzalez."

"Oh, I remember him—he's the computer nerd, right? Always got his head in his cell phone."

"Yes, that's the one, Dani. Anyway, I would like you to talk with him."

"Talk with him?" asked Dan. "About what? What's the problem?"

"He is doing something online that is making him money. I don't understand it, but suddenly he has a bank account and new clothes. I don't want to ask because, you know, if I find out he's doing something illegal, well... I would have to arrest him, and he is family, and I don't want to arrest him... so you see, I am in a funny position. That's why I would like you to talk to him and find out what he is doing. And if it's something illegal, I don't want to know about it. But I want you to stop him. You have my permission to use any means necessary to stop him. I will not have a nephew of mine getting mixed up in crime."

Dan nodded. "Okay, I can try. But what if he won't open up to me?"

"As I said, Dani, you can use any means necessary. If he won't tell you what he's doing, take him out to the woods and beat him until he does. It's like the Bible says, 'Use the rod to beat the child.' I usually find that works well with prisoners. It will work with Hector."

"I don't think that's what the Bible says," Dan replied. "But I will have a little talk with him."

"Thank you, Dani. He goes to some computer club after school. It meets at the House of Culture, next to the Parque Central. He usually gets out of that meeting around four in the afternoon. You can catch him there this afternoon as he's leaving."

"I see that you have thought this thing out," Dan said.

"Details beat the Devil," don Fernando said.

"I don't know what that means," Dan replied.

"I don't know either, Dani, but it's in the Bible, so I know it's true."

And so it was that that very afternoon, when the Hector was leaving his meeting with the Computer Club at Villa Rosario's House of Culture, that Dan was sitting on one of the concrete park benches, waiting for him. Now, lest you get the wrong impression, I should explain that the House of Culture—or Casa de la Cultura, as it's known in Spanish—is just an old annex building of the Catholic Church, which is situated next to the Parque Central. The building has a room full of old donated computers and another room full of art supplies. The town offers art classes and basic computer programming classes there. These are after-school activities designed to give the school kids something to do, you know, to keep them occupied, so they don't do drugs. But the town also allows the kids to organize their own meetings there, and some of the older kids, including Hector, had organized a Computer Club as place to come and share new programming skills. So, anyway, Hector was leaving the House of Culture when Dan spotted him and waved him over to the bench where he was sitting.

Dan noticed right away that Hector was wearing brand new tennis shoes, and they weren't the cheap Chinese knock-off tennis shoes that the stores in Villa Rosario sold. These looked like authentic Nike-brand shoes.

Hector greeted Dan with the traditional Spanish term of respect of "don," which is how a younger person in Panama refers to an older person. "Hola, don Dan," he said. "How are you?"

"I am good, Hector. Looks like you got some new shoes."

Hector smiled. "Yes, I just bought them yesterday. I had to go all the way to La Chorrera to find them. They are very cool."

"Sit down, Hector," Dan said, "I want to talk to you for a minute."

Hector slipped off his backpack and sat down on the concrete bench and looked at Dan.

"Hector," Dan began, "you know how gringos are direct? How we always try to go straight to the point of something? How we don't like to beat around the bush?"

Now, to be clear, dear Reader, Dan and Hector were talking in Spanish, so I've taken some liberties with the translation. Dan actually used the phrase "andar en floreos" which literally translates "to walk in flourishes," but it means the same thing as the English expression "to beat around the bush." The point is, Hector understood Dan's question.

So Hector nodded yes, and Dan continued. "Well, your uncle don Fernando asked me to talk to you. He has become aware that recently you seem to have money. And he wants to know how this happened. He wants to know where and how you are getting this money."

"Oh," said Hector, "that is easy to explain. I've been selling bitcoin."

Dan looked at Hector, and for a tiny micro-second his brain didn't understand what he had just heard. Here was a fifteen-year-old boy, telling him that he was selling bitcoin. During that mini-micro-second, the words that were reaching Dan's ears didn't match up with the boyish image that was being transmitted into his brain by his eyes. Dan blinked and said, "You're selling bitcoin?"

"Well, not real bitcoin," Hector said. "I'm selling used bitcoin. I have a website, and I sell used bitcoin on it, and people send me money."

Once again, Dan had that experience of his brain freezing up just for the briefest of micro-seconds. "Wha-what is a *used* bitcoin, Hector?" he asked.

"Here, I will show you," Hector said and pulled open his backpack and took out a manila folder. "I have this website called worthlesscyptocurrency.com, and I sell used bitcoin on it. Here's a picture of the home page of the website."

Hector handed Dan a sheet of paper. It appeared to be a screenshot of a website, and as Hector had just said, the website was called worthlesscryptocurrency. com. Below the website's name were the bold letters *Buy Used Bitcoin*, and then there were three links with the captions: *What is a NNFT?* and *Place Your Order* and *Track Your Purchase.* In the middle of the page was some sort of financial chart in bright blue, that showed an arrow going up diagonally across the graph. Finally, near the bottom there was another set of bold letters that proclaimed: *Watch Your Interest Grow!*

Dan stared at the paper, trying to make sense out of it. Finally, he looked up at Hector and asked, "This is your website?"

Hector nodded proudly. "Yup."

"And people send you money?"

Hector smiled broadly. "They sure do."

Dan frowned and said, "Hector, is this legal?"

"Oh, it's totally legal, don Dan. See, there's a disclaimer at the very bottom of the page."

Dan looked down at the bottom of the page. Indeed, there was a paragraph, in tiny print, that read: "Legal Disclaimer: Worthlesscryptocurrency.com is the official website of Worthless Cryptocurrency (WCC), a limited liability corporation registered in Panama. WCC is not a bank nor a financial institution. All postings and comments are for entertainment value only. *Used Bitcoin* is a term of art that refers to a NNFT created by WCC. NNFTs are non-nonfungible tokens that have no intrinsic value. NNFTs are not an investment. However, their uniqueness may generate personal interest among interested parties. WCC asserts no promises nor responsibility for financial gain or losses for NNFT players. Play intelligently. See our Terms of Service for details."

Dan read it twice. "This is legal gobbledygook, Hector. What does it mean?

"It means that I'm not responsible." Hector replied. "Señor Ricardo Mendes wrote that for me."

"*Ricardo* wrote this for you? So, *he knows* about this?!"

"Oh, yes," Hector said. "Señor Ricardo was a lawyer back in the United States, you know."

"Yes-yes-yes, I know. Okay, let's back up, Hector. I want to understand this. This… this website" Dan said, shaking the sheet of paper, "who created this website?

"I did," Hector said proudly. "Well… Carlos Wang helped me some, but the idea was mine."

"Wait… *Carlos Wang* helped you?" Dan asked. "So, Carlos knows about this, too?!"

"Oh, sure. He knows all about it."

"Okay… so you and Carlos own this website?" Dan asked.

"Oh no, WCC owns the website."

"Oh-kay," Dan said slowly. "And WCC is a limited liability corporation here in Panama?"

"Uh-huh."

"And did Ricardo help you set that up?"

"Uh-huh."

"And who owns WCC?" Dan asked.

"Oh, it's owned by a shell company called Worldwide Worthless Cryptocurrency."

"Of course it is," said Dan. "And I suppose Ricardo helped you set that up as well."

"Yup."

"And who owns this shell company?"

"Well," Hector paused then said, "there's some layers… but basically, I do."

"You and you alone?"

Hector nodded his head yes. "There are some proxy directors... but basically, I own it."

"And what does this WCC company do, Hector?"

Hector's brow furrowed a bit. "Well, it doesn't really do anything, don Dan. The way that señor Ricardo explained it to me was that WCC *holds* the website; it owns the website, and the website sells used bitcoin."

"And what exactly is a used bitcoin, Hector?" Dan asked.

Hector smiled broadly. "It's something I made up, don Dan. You know how a bitcoin is basically just made of numbers, right? I mean, it's just binary code, and binary code is just a string of numbers on a computer. Well, one day, I was looking at some old coins, some *real* metal coins, and they were all worn down, smooth around the edges. And I started to wonder what a bitcoin would look like once it was used up, you know. And I decided that the numbers couldn't be worn down, you know, because they exist on a computer. So, I decided that a *used* bitcoin would have to be its last known address, assuming it never moved again. So I bought some satoshis and put them in my crypto wallet, and then I offered NNFTs of them for sale and called them *used bitcoins*... and people bought them... so I created some more NNFTs of them and offered *them* for sale... and people bought them, too... and the business kind of grew..."

Dan's head shook involuntarily. Finally, he asked, "What's a satoshi?"

"A satoshi is a hundred millionth of a bitcoin, don Dan. It's the smallest fraction of a bitcoin that you can buy. It's named after Satoshi Nakamoto, the founder of bitcoin."

"So, you're selling these... these... these tiny fractions of bitcoin?" Dan sputtered. "Basically, you're selling bitcoin?"

"No, don Dan. I'm selling an NNFT of the last known address of a fraction of a bitcoin. I don't actually transfer the satoshis. I keep them in my crypto wallet."

Dan was still trying to understand exactly what Hector was saying. "You *keep* these satoshis—these bitcoin fractions?" Dan asked.

"Well, yes, of course," Hector replied. "If I transferred them to the buyer, then they wouldn't be used. They would be valid crypto currency, and the other person could spend them. They would be *usable*, not *used*."

Dan exhaled slowly. "Okay, okay, I think I understand... you're selling NFTs of these... these satoshis, right? I've heard of NFTs. They're like a digital picture of something, right? So, you're selling a digital picture of a fraction of a bitcoin that is in your wallet."

"No, I don't sell NFTs. I sell NNFTs, which are non-nonfungible tokens."

Dan head made another involuntary shake. "And what the hell is that?"

"It's something that señor Ricardo and I came up with. Señor Ricardo said that I needed something easy to transfer out of my crypto wallet to someone else's crypto wallet so I would have something to sell, because I needed to keep the actual satoshi *in* my wallet, you see? We thought about using a hash value. But señor Ricardo said that wouldn't work because a hash value is not unique. And we couldn't use NFTs because you can't have two NFTs of the exact same satoshi, so..."

"Wait, stop stop stop," interrupted Dan. "You lost me. I'm not a computer person, Hector. Let me just understand the basics. I have to be able to explain this to your uncle. You have a website... And you are selling pictures of tiny fractions of bitcoins through this website.... And people are buying those pictures, and that's how you're making this money, and... and Ricardo Mendes says it's all legal. Is that... is that basically what's going on?"

"Sí, don Dan. That's what I am doing."

"Okay, okay… and how are people paying you?"

"They pay in cryptocurrency. I take Bitcoin, Ethereum, Dogecoin, Stablecoin… pretty much any crypto token."

"I mean, *how* do they *send* you cryptocurrency?" Dan asked.

"I have an account on CIE," Hector answered.

Dan sighed. "And what is CIE, Hector?"

"That's Coinbase International Exchange. It's a bitcoin exchange located in Bermuda. It's a platform for exchanging cryptocurrency. I have, or rather, WCC has, an account there, and clients pay me on that account."

Once again, Dan's brain had to correlate the image of a fifteen-year-old boy sitting in front of him saying that he had a bitcoin account on some international exchange located in Bermuda.

"You have an account on a cryptocurrency exchange?" Dan asked.

"Well, WCC does. Señor Ricardo helped me set it up."

"Right," Dan said slowly. "Ricardo helped you." Dan decided that he needed to talk with his friend Ricardo Mendes.

"Okay, Hector," Dan said. "Let me say this out loud, just to make sure I understand it: Ricardo Mendes helped you set up a shell company, so that you can buy tiny fractions of bitcoin; and then, you take some kind of a digital picture of these tiny fractions; and you sell these pictures on a website that Carlos Wang helped you design; and people buy these pictures; and they send money to you through this crypto exchange place that's in Bermuda… is that basically accurate?"

"Sí, don Dan."

"Okay, okay," Dan said. "And Ricardo says this is all totally legal?"

Hector nodded his head yes.

"Okay, I think I understand." Dan paused and thought for a moment, and then, as an afterthought, asked. "And the money that people send you—all these different cryptocurrencies—you keep them in some sort of savings account on this bitcoin exchange?"

"Oh no, don Dan. As soon as someone pays me, I convert their cryptocurrency to US dollars and transfer it out of the CIE exchange to my bank account here in Villa Rosario."

Dan tried to process Hector's answer. "And you do that because...?" Dan asked.

"Well, don Dan, cryptocurrency is not a safe place to keep money."

Dan's brain started to hurt. He had assumed that this teenager was one of the millions of young ardent believers in cryptocurrency, and that that was why he was involved in this project.

"Wait a minute, Hector. You are selling bitcoin to people, but you don't believe bitcoin is safe?"

"Oh no, don Dan. Cryptocurrency is worthless. That's why I call my website worthless cryptocurrency dot com. Don Ricardo calls bitcoin a self-perpetuating Ponzi scheme, and I agree with that. The only cryptocurrency I hold are the satoshi coins that I keep, so I can sell their NNFTs as used bitcoins."

"Wait... this bitcoin project is your business," Dan sputtered, "but you don't believe in bitcoin?"

"Well, don Ricardo once told me that the owners of casinos never gamble. He said the smart casino owner is rich because he knows that gamblers always lose. He says that I'm like the owner of a casino. Don Ricardo says I'm in the entertainment business, not the bitcoin business."

Dan closed his eyes and took a deep breath. Then he opened his eyes and said, "Okay, Hector. Well, I thank you for explaining all this to me. Your uncle was concerned that you were doing something illegal. I'm going to talk with Ricardo, but as far as I can understand it, you are not doing anything illegal. It's *incomprehensible* to me, but not illegal. And you are making money at this?"

"Oh yes, don Dan," Hector said and pointed at his new shoes. "The business is doing well. These shoes cost me $200 in La Chorrera."

"Yes, okay, Hector. I'm going to try and absorb everything you told me. I may have more questions tomorrow, if that's okay. Does your Computer Club meet tomorrow afternoon?

"Yes, don Dan, it meets every day after school."

"Okay, well, I may come back tomorrow. Thank you again for explaining this to me. It's okay if I explain all this to your uncle?"

"It is no problem, don Dan."

And with that, Dan stood up and walked out of the park. His head was jammed full of thoughts, but he also felt depressed. Cryptocurrency was a brave new world, but Dan didn't understand it, and he was clearly not a part of it. He headed in the direction of Ricardo's apartment and hoped that Ricardo would be at home.

CHAPTER THREE

I should probably pause here, dear Reader, and say a few words about expats, which as you know, is short for expatriate—a person who, for whatever reason, has chosen to live their life outside of their native country. Dan Landes is an expatriate, and so is Ricardo Mendes. Ricardo, despite his Latino-sounding name, is a citizen of the United States. He was born in the United States, grew up in the United States, became a lawyer in the United States, until fate, or destiny, or his own wanderlust, brought him to Panama. Likewise for Dan Landes, who was a police detective in the Crenshaw district of Los Angeles, until he took early retirement and moved to Panama. How they each got to Panama, and how they met and became friends, is a story for another day. The important fact here is that they both are expats.

To be an expat, at its most basic core, means that you don't belong. It means that you left your native country because you felt that you didn't belong there, and then you traveled to another country—or countries—where you try to fit in, where you try and create a new home. But you can't, because you are not a native to that country and its culture. No matter how hard an expat tries, he will always be a foreigner—or *extranjero*, as they say in Panama—to the country he has moved to. Cultures are simply different, and if you were not born into a certain culture, if you were not initiated and indoctrinated into that culture at an early age, you will never fully and truly understand that culture. And you will never be accepted into that culture by the locals, no matter how broadly they smile. An expat can live for forty years in another country, and he will always be a foreigner. It's just the way it is. I don't make the rules.

And in fact, one of the reasons that Dan was walking over to Ricardo's apartment that afternoon is that he wanted to hear Ricardo's explanation of Hector's bitcoin business. It didn't matter that Hector had just told him clearly and honestly exactly what he was doing, Dan still needed to hear the explanation from another native-born North American before he could really understand it. Plus, Dan needed to hear that explanation in English. Even though Dan was fluent in Spanish, there is always a subtlety and depth to your own native language that makes for true understanding. Also, Dan and Ricardo had been friends in Panama for more than a decade; and friendship, as you know, dear Reader, creates a certain trust in, and understanding of, the words that the other person is using. A simple sentence between friends conveys more meaning and understanding than a whole paragraph between strangers.

Luckily for Dan, Ricardo was at home. Dan found him sitting at a small table on his balcony, enjoying a cup of coffee and working on his laptop computer. After a round of greetings, including apologies from Dan for showing up unannounced, and offers of coffee, and acceptance of offers, the two men sat down on the balcony and Dan got to the matter at hand.

"Can you explain to me," Dan asked, "in simple terms, what the hell Hector Gonzalez is doing with this bitcoin thing?"

Ricardo laughed. "Oh, that kid, he's quite a wiz, isn't he? He may be a bit socially awkward, but he's a genius on the internet. Did you know that he teaches a computer class after school at the House of Culture, and that even adults take classes there from him?"

"Yes, I just came from talking to him there," Dan replied. "And he was telling me all about his website. He says you helped set that up for him."

"Not the website," Ricardo said, "just the corporate veil around the website. He's getting quite a good legal education with this project of his. I think he could be a good lawyer one day. Anyway, Carlos Wang sent him to me. He and Carlos were building this website, you see, to sell these, um, *used bitcoins*, as he calls them. Carlos thought Hector needed some legal protection—which he absolutely did, you know—to hide his identity. So, Carlos sent him to me, and I helped him set up a couple of LLCs—you know, limited liability corporations—to shield him. We incorporated his Worthless Cryptocurrency LLC here in Panama, and then we put that under another LLC, called Worldwide Worthless Cryptocurrency, which we incorporated in Bermuda. We chose Bermuda because they have great privacy laws, but also because Coinbase has their international bitcoin exchange incorporated there. So it made it easier for him to open a bitcoin account there."

"He's *fifteen*, Ricardo! How can he open up an account?"

"Well, *he* doesn't have the account; the corporation does. Coinbase doesn't know that he's fifteen. As far as they are concerned, they are just dealing with another anonymous company that holds bitcoin. There are millions of such companies registered in Bermuda, and probably a lot of them are being run by teenagers." Ricardo gave a little laugh.

"And why is he using Coinbase in Bermuda?" Dan asked.

"Well, to be honest, the only reason we chose them is because I had set up LLCs in Bermuda before. Hector needed an offshore corporation to hide his ownership. I could have picked Aruba, or the Bahamas, or any number of places. But I was familiar with Bermuda from when I had my law practice in New York. I used to set up LLCs for my New York clients there, so I still had all the forms. And when I discovered that Coinbase was also incorporated there, well... then, it was a no-brainer. I just had his LLC open up an account with Coinbase, and Carlos helped him configure the account so he could receive different types of cryptocurrencies there. Carlos arranged it so that any crypto he received was instantly converted to US dollars and transferred to his bank account here. Well, actually, it goes through a bank in Bermuda first, but eventually it ends up here. He has to pay an extra commission to Coinbase for this. Still, we all agreed it was worth it. And he already had a bank account here because his dad had set it up for him years ago. And there's no taxes to pay, because the money is all earned outside of Panama. So, all of that was pretty easy."

"But why does he need LLCs? I mean, why does he need to hide his identity?" Dan asked.

"Oh, well, the internet has become a very dangerous place, Dan. It's not like years ago when you and I were learning how to email, and Facebook and MySpace were the only game in town. No, no, no. Now, the internet is full of millions and millions of bad actors, looking to rob anyone. And it doesn't matter whether you have money or not. For example, Japan has this big problem now with scammers targeting young girls in social media, downloading the photos that these girls post of themselves, and then using AI to convert those photos into porn and then blackmailing these poor teenagers with this fake porn. I told Hector that it didn't matter if his project was successful or not, we *had to* keep *his identity* off the internet. There's *nothing* that connects him with his used bitcoin website. I told him at the very beginning that if he was going to go online and offer anything for sale, that he was basically presenting himself as a target for internet hackers and thieves."

"And *what* is he actually selling?" Dan asked.

"Well, it's a bit complicated. Carlos can probably explain it better than I can, but basically, he's selling a digital address of a fraction of a bitcoin, along with the promise that he will never move that bitcoin—that it will never be spent— and he calls that digital address a *used* bitcoin, meaning it's *used-up,* so it can never be transferred or used as payment."

"And why would anyone buy that?" Dan asked.

Ricardo shrugged. "It's a gimmick. But then... so is bitcoin. I mean, anyone can create a crypto token, a bitcoin knockoff... and that's kinda what this is. Did you know that there are over twenty thousand different types of cryptocurrencies floating around the internet now? And that doesn't include NFTs, which are another type of crypto token. If you counted all the different types of crypto tokens that exist... well shit, there's probably a billion of them. But somehow, for whatever reason, some of them become more popular than others, and people buy them. Remember the Bored Apes NFTs? Sold for thousands of dollars each. Remember One Coin? It wasn't even on a blockchain—wasn't even a real cryptocurrency, but they sold four billion dollars-worth of them. It's a crazy world, Dan—but it's no different than when we were kids. Remember Pet Rocks? They were basically rocks that were marketed as pets! But people bought them. Remember baseball trading cards? Sold for thousands of dollars! But they were just pictures of baseball players! If someone thinks something is valuable, they'll buy it!"

Ricardo paused for a second, then continued, "But I told Hector and Carlos that this project had to be totally legal, that I wasn't going to help them if there was any fraud involved. That's why we named the company Worthless Cryptocurrency, and that's why we have a disclaimer on the website. Shit, you should see the Terms of Service Agreement that customers have to sign in order to buy a used bitcoin. It took me days to write that! But it basically says that they understand that they are buying something of zero value."

"And yet... people are buying these things?" Dan asked.

Ricardo nodded. "Evidently, they are selling well."

"Why?"

Ricardo shrugged again. "People are crazy, Dan. Remember beanie babies? Remember hula hoops?"

"Are people buying them only because they think they will go up in value?" Dan asked.

"Oh, absolutely."

"Will they?"

"Hector's already raised the selling price three times," Ricardo replied. "People are already starting to trade and resell them."

"Jesus," Dan said. "Okay, so let me see if I've got this straight: Hector is buying these... these satoshis, he calls them—these fractions of a bitcoin. And then he makes an NFT of them..."

"No," said Ricardo, interrupting Dan. "It's not an NFT, it's an NNFT. There's a difference."

"Jesus," Dan said again. "Okay... you know, I really don't understand this NFT stuff. Can you explain it to me?"

"Well," Ricardo began, "an NFT is a non-fungible token..."

"No, no," interrupted Dan. "I mean explain it to me in a way I can understand."

Ricardo paused to think, and then said. "Okay. Suppose you have a document, like a birth certificate. And you have an original, all properly notarized and everything, okay? And you make a copy of it, like on a Xerox machine. In fact, you make a hundred copies of it. And suppose you give a copy to someone for some legal purpose, okay? In fact, suppose you give all one hundred copies out to various people... but you keep the original birth certificate, and you tell everyone that you've got the original, and that you've only given them a copy, okay? Now, what's the value of the copy? Its value is only to indicate that the original exists, right? I mean, it has value, but only because it's evidence that an original exists. I mean, you couldn't sell it. A copy has no value in the general marketplace, but it might be important when applying for a passport or something. You with me so far?"

Dan nodded.

"Okay," Ricardo continued, " Now, let's take this example a step further. Suppose you *scan* that original birth certificate into your computer and create a PDF of it and save it in a file on your computer. You've created PDFs on your computer before, right? So, you scan this original birth certificate into your computer; you save it as a PDF; and you email this PDF to someone as an attachment, okay? And they can click on that attachment and open the PDF and read it. And the reason you sent them a PDF is so they can't alter it—I mean, *theoretically*, they can't alter it. That was the original purpose of the PDF. The person you send it to can only open it and read it or print it. And you still have the original hard copy birth certificate, right? And you still have the original PDF of that birth certificate that you created on your computer.

"Okay, good. Now, the reality is, that people *can* alter PDFs, so someone could receive the PDF that you send them, and they could alter it. So now, suppose that now you *are worried* that somebody will alter your PDF, so much so that you don't want to email it out. So... suppose you take that PDF, and you put it on a *blockchain*, and for purposes of this explanation, let's just assume that a blockchain is like Facebook or Craigslist or Instagram—that it's just a public place where people can post stuff. And so you put this PDF on the blockchain, and instead of emailing the PDF out, you just email the *address* of where that PDF is on the blockchain, so that people can click on that address, and they will go to the blockchain and they can see the PDF, and they could print out a copy, but they can't alter the PDF that is at that address. You still with me? Okay, that technology exists today. You can put a document on a blockchain and send someone the address, and that address is called a *hash value*; and someone could click on that hash value and look at your document, but they can't alter your document. That hash value is like the xerox copy of your birth certificate. Its only value is to indicate that you have the original birth certificate. It has no intrinsic value other than that. You can't sell a hash value in the marketplace. You still with me?

Dan nodded again.

"Okay," Ricardo continued, "Now, let me alter the example. Suppose an artist paints a portrait of something. And suppose this artist is very good—famous good—and the painting is actually worth something. Okay, you know how you can make a *print* of a painting? You see it all the time in art stores—where a print is marked something like... fourteen slash three hundred, meaning that they made three hundred prints of this painting and you are buying the fourteenth print, right? And that print is worth something because they only printed three hundred of them, okay? Well, suppose they only made *one print* of that painting—just one! And suppose that print comes with a certificate from the painter or the art store that swears that this is the *only* print that exists of the original painting. That would make the print more valuable, right? Because it's the *only* print of that painting, and it comes with a certificate that says it's the only print. Well, that's what an NFT is. It's a digital copy of something that certifies that it's the only copy of that thing.

"So, anyway, Hector comes to me, and he's explaining this used bitcoin project. He's bought some satoshis—these tiny fractions of a bitcoin—and he wants to sell them as quote-*used*-unquote, right? Originally, he tells me he wants to sell hash values of them—that is, he just wants to sell the address of where this satoshi is on the blockchain. And I tell him no. I suggest to him that a hash value isn't valuable enough; it isn't unique enough. It's just an address. And he can't sell an NFT of the satoshi, because an NFT, by definition, is the *only* copy of the satoshi, and he wants to make and sell multiple copies of the same satoshi. So, we come up with the concept of an NNFT—a non-NFT. It's like an NFT in that it comes with a certificate saying that it's an official copy of the satoshi—it's like that print of a painting—but it's *not the only* print. It's like a hash value, in that it gives the address of the satoshi on the block chain, but it can't be copied. It's unique. It's like an NFT in that respect, but the difference is that Hector can make multiple copies of the *same* satoshi. He's only got about a dozen satoshis, but this way he can create multiple... official... used... bitcoins out of each one."

Dan just stared at Ricardo. Finally, he said, "Are you saying that all he's doing is selling a picture of a satoshi with a certificate saying that it's an *official* copy? That's it? He's just creating bunches of these official copies and selling them?"

"Pretty much... but don't forget, Dan, that these official copies come with a promise that he will never sell the original satoshi. The customer can rest assured that he has purchased an *official* used bitcoin, and that the original will never be sold or traded again."

"But, Ricardo, that's... that's just bullshit. Why would anyone buy that?"

"Oh Dan, you don't know the immense scale of official memorabilia!" exclaimed Ricardo, shaking his head. "Think of all the rock stars selling official T-shirts at their concerts; think of all the sports teams selling official baseball jerseys and official footballs at department stores; think of old vinyl phonograph records, think of authentic Tiffany lamps made in Tiffany factories, think of antique stores full of collectable plates; think of governments issuing collectible coins... The collectibles market is worth billions, Dan, *billions*."

"But these used bitcoins are not worth anything, Ricardo," Dan protested.

Ricardo laughed. "Well, of course they are. Value is in the eye of the beholder. A used bitcoin is worth whatever someone will pay for it. I had an aunt, back in New York, who used to collect these porcelain plates that had pictures of Elvis on them. She must have had a hundred of them, all framed and hung on her wall, or in display cases. She thought the money she spent on them was well spent."

"But at least that was something she could look at," Dan responded. "She could decorate with it, show it to her friends. It sounds to me that the people who are buying Hector's used bitcoins are just speculating. They are just buying them hoping they go up in value and that they can sell them."

"Well, that's true," Ricardo admitted. "That's pretty much the only reason they sell."

"So they're just bullshit," Dan repeated.

"Well, as clearly stated in the official disclaimer and in the Terms of Use, they have no intrinsic value. But, that said, neither does an Elvis plate. And yet, people still buy them."

Dan just shook his head, then asked, "How much money is he making on this venture?"

"I'm not sure where things stand today. He had a lot of upfront costs, in terms of advertising. He had to make a bunch of videos for YouTube; and he had to pay some influencers to talk about used bitcoin on their podcasts; and he took out some ads on the Crypto Times, Coin Telegram, and CoinDesk…"

Dan looked confused, so Ricardo added, "Those are crypto news websites. Anyway, he finally broke even last week. The money is just starting to trickle in. Hector was all proud that he actually was making a profit. He told me the other day he was really hoping it would skyrocket this week."

"Do you think that will happen?" Dan asked.

Ricardo shrugged. "Between you and me, Dan, I doubt it. There are millions of crypto tokens being created each week. I doubt that his will stand out. But, it's harmless, and it's educational for him."

"And there's no chance he can get into trouble with this?" Dan asked.

"I don't think so. I mean, from a legal standpoint, we made it as clear as possible that this was not an investment of any kind. I think he's safe. Besides, it's Panama. What could happen?"

Dan nodded. "Okay, well, thanks Ricardo, I appreciate the information. Don Fernando had asked me to look into it. He was kind of worried that maybe Hector was getting involved with drugs, and that that was where he was getting his new cash."

"Nah," said Ricardo. "You can tell don Fernando not to worry. Hector is a good kid. He's just doing what all fifteen-year-olds do—he's exploring his world and expanding his horizons. The only difference is that his world is all created inside a computer, or rather, inside a million computers that are all connected to each other on the internet."

"Yeah," said Dan. "Anyway, I'm going to head down to the police station and see if I can catch don Fernando before he goes home for the day, so I can try to explain all this to him," Dan said.

CHAPTER FOUR

As Dan was walking through the town of Villa Rosario, hoping to catch don Fernando still in his office at the police station, other events were happening in the world. The world is a big place, isn't it? And, at any given moment, billions of things are happening all at once elsewhere in the world, but usually none of them affect us directly. Most of us, dear Reader, are rather like flat-earthers, aren't we? We think that the world we see in front of us is the only world there is, and that nothing else really matters. And most of the time, that's true. Dan was walking towards the Parque Central, next to the large Catholic church, heading to the police station on the opposite side of the park. The sun was beginning to set, and large birds were calling to each other from the tops of the palm trees that line the Parque Central. Dan was mulling over all the things that Hector had told him, and all the things that Ricardo had told him. He felt confident that he could reassure don Fernando that his nephew Hector was not doing anything illegal, and that this project was just a little fad that would probably go the way of all things. In fact, this whole bitcoin enterprise of Hector's might actually be educational for the teenager. Maybe, Dan thought, Hector could refer to it when he applied to the university in a few years. At any rate, Dan felt that he had completed the task that don Fernando had asked him to do. He had talked with Hector, and he had verified that everything Hector had told him was true. So he could reassure don Fernando, and then Dan's work would be done, and he could return to his quiet life as a gringo in Villa Rosario.

But sometimes, dear Reader, occasionally, every now and then, every once in a blue moon, the events that happen in this big world of ours *do* affect us, or affect people around us; and at the exact moment that Dan was walking through the Parque Central, there were events happening in other parts of the world that would definitely affect him and the people around him.

The first thing that was happening at that exact moment was that a social media influencer named Gloria María Hernández was doing a podcast in Los Angeles, California. Gloria Hernández was a well-known crypto social media personality in the Latino bitcoin circles. Besides pumping out a ton of YouTube videos, she ran a daily live podcast where she talked endlessly and enthusiastically about how bitcoin was going to change the world. She was young, pretty, sexy, upbeat, charming and charismatic, which made her the perfect spokesperson for a variety of financial technology enterprises—known as "fin-tech" companies—that were looking to promote whatever product they were trying to sell. In other words, she was a whore, or, as she was often described in the United States, an astute businesswoman. She didn't make any money from bitcoin herself; rather, she made thousands of dollars each month sponsoring various cryptocurrency tokens, or apps, or devices, and her words were scooped up immediately by her throngs of devoted listeners. And, as it just so happened, Hector Gonzalez had paid her a sizable fee to talk about his fabulous used bitcoin project, which is exactly what she was doing on this particular afternoon as Dan was walking through the park.

Dan was blissfully unaware of this, of course. But at that exact moment, Gloria was saying breathlessly into the microphone, "This new token, these *used bitcoins* are absolutely going to explode this week! I want you to share this podcast with all your friends, because you don't want to get rich alone! If you like making money, then you should definitely buy these used bitcoins. They are amazingly affordable now, but they won't be for long! I've been buying and selling cryptocurrency for years, and most people who talk about crypto don't know what they are talking about, *but I do*, my friends. And *I am telling you*, my friends, used bitcoins are going to go through the roof. Let me give you their website name. Their website is worthlesscryptocurrency. com. I *love* their sense of humor! You can use my affiliate link to get a ten percent discount off your first purchase. Do it today, because these tokens are going to take off."

It's probably a good thing that Dan was completely oblivious to Gloria's sales pitch, as he would have found her positive attitude and over-the-top enthusiasm very annoying, and he would have found her promises of financial gain rather alarming. Of course, Gloria couldn't care less what people like Dan thought. She had simply agreed to promote Hector's used bitcoin and had already deposited his money into her bank account. Gloria was always happy to promote anything crypto-related. It's how she made her living. She brought the same chipper attitude and energetic language to every crypto token. She had done it so often and for so long that it was an automatic presentation for her. She had no real idea what Hector's used bitcoins were about.

And at the exact same moment that Gloria María Hernández was expounding exuberantly about used bitcoins on her podcast in California, another social media influencer in Florida named Roger Van Kette was uploading his most recent crypto video onto YouTube. Like Gloria, Roger Van Kette was a crypto influencer. Unlike Gloria, Roger had a specific demographic. His motto was "Christians for Crypto," and his logo was consisted of a cross with a large bitcoin symbol at the top. This idolatry might be easily dismissed except for the fact that Roger had over five million followers. His videos were professionally made; he had the voice and charisma of a Baptist televangelist; and he posted new videos on social media every day. His devoted followers shared these videos with their friends, and the cumulative effect was that his videos often reached ten million views each day. Like Gloria, Roger Van Kette did not own any cryptocurrency himself, despite his claims in his videos that he did. Roger preferred good old American cash, and his annual income ran into the millions. And just like Gloria, Roger was a whore, meaning that he would happily sponsor any new crypto token if he was paid to do so. And, as it happened, Hector Gonzalez had paid Roger to do so. Roger's new video was all about the great potential of used bitcoins, and just like Gloria, Roger had no idea what Hector's used bitcoins were really about; and just like Gloria, he didn't care.

On the other hand, there were two people who had a much clearer idea of the potential for Hector's used bitcoins, and those two people were the Lukov brothers. The Lukov brothers' given names were Georgi and Dimitar, but since they were twins and impossible to tell apart, people just called them the Lukov brothers. Like Gloria and Roger, they were into crypto; but unlike Gloria and Roger, they actually bought and sold crypto... or, to be more accurate, they pumped and dumped crypto. They were originally from Bulgaria, but they had made the town of Zug, Switzerland, their homebase for the past several years. Switzerland is a crypto-friendly country, and the town of Zug, in particular, is very crypto-positive, so it was natural for the Lukov brothers to set up shop there. And their business model, or to be accurate, their fraud model, was to find new crypto tokens that were trending, invest heavily into them for anywhere from a few minutes to a few days, and then dump them as soon as they began to rise in popularity. Normally, this would be considered speculation, which is foolish but legal. But, what the Lukov brothers did that made it illegal was that they pumped up their chosen investment by sending out fake press releases and forged government documents that gave the selected crypto token an aura of legitimacy. For example, when the infamous Zimmer coin came out, the Lukov brothers issued a press release that looked like it was issued by the government of El Salvador saying that it was going to adopt the Zimmer coin as an official currency. The token shot up in value for a few hours until El Salvador denounced the hoax, but by then the Lukov brothers had cashed out their investment and netted approximately four hundred thousand dollars in profit.

And so it was that at the exact moment that Dan was walking into the Villa Rosario police department, the Lukov brothers had just finished listening to Gloria María Hernández's podcast on Hector's used bitcoin, and they were discussing how they could take advantage of this new twist in crypto tokens.

But as I said, Dan was blissfully unaware of these things, which was probably a good thing. If each of us was aware of all the things occurring at this exact moment that were going to affect us, well... we wouldn't be able to get through our day. We'd be frozen in our chairs in fear, waiting for the next shoe to drop. But we are not aware of these things, so we manage to make our way.

And so, at this exact moment, Dan was entering the police station. He waved at the desk sergeant, who just nodded his head in the direction of don Fernando's office, indicating that don Fernando was still there. And Dan walked down the hallway to don Fernando's open door.

"Ah Dani," don Fernando said when he looked up, "what a pleasant surprise. Come in, come in."

Dan smiled and stepped into the office and took a seat at the large chair in front of don Fernando's desk.

"I just dropped by to update you on your nephew Hector," Dan said.

"Ah, yes, please," don Fernando said. "Tell me everything."

"I spoke with him today, and I can tell you that he is making his money legally. It's very complicated, but everything he is doing is above board."

"What does this mean, *above board*?"

"It means that he's legal. What he's doing is okay."

"Oh, good, Dani. I was worried. But tell me, what *exactly* is he doing? His father tells me he has a lot of money."

"Okay, I'm going to try and explain," Dan said. "You've heard about bitcoin, right? What he's doing... well, it's kind of hard to explain, but basically, it's like he's buying and selling bitcoin... although he's not actually selling the bitcoin itself..."

Dan paused. It dawned on him that this was going to be harder to explain than he had thought. "What I mean, don Fernando, is that he's buying bitcoin... well, not whole bitcoins, but just tiny fractions of bitcoin... and he doesn't sell them... but it's kind of like he takes a picture of them and sells the pictures as... well, kind of like souvenirs..."

"I don't understand, Dani."

"Well, you know how some people collect old coins, don Fernando? They collect them because they think they are valuable? Well, it's like Hector has bought some old coins, and he's selling pictures of them on the internet, and for some reason other people like these pictures, even though they are just pictures of a coin. And so they are... they are buying them. They send him money for these pictures..."

Don Fernando nodded his head slowly. "That does not make any sense, Dani."

"Okay, let me try to explain this another way. Hector had this idea for a business, a business that sold these digital pictures of pieces of bitcoin, and so he talked to Carlos Wang, and Carlos thought it was a good idea, so Carlos helped him create a website to sell these pictures..."

"The same Carlos who works for me?" interrupted don Fernando.

"Yes," Dan continued. "So Carlos helped him to set up a website in order to sell these pictures. And just to be safe, Carlos took Hector over to meet Ricardo Mendes, and Ricardo also thought Hector's project was a good one, so Ricardo helped him set up a corporation to protect his website..."

Don Fernando interrupted Dan again. "*Both* Carlos *and* Ricardo helped him with this?"

"Yes," Dan said. "They both thought it was a good business idea. So Carlos is helping him with the technical part of the business, and Ricardo is helping him with the legal side of the business..."

"Hang on a second, Dani," don Fernando said, and he pressed the intercom button on his desk. When the desk sergeant answered, don Fernando said, "Sergeant, could you do me a favor and find Carlos Wang and ask him to come to my office?"

"Sí, Capitán," came the reply over the small black box.

"So, Hector is selling photographs of money? Is that what he's doing?" don Fernando asked with a confused frown on his face.

"Kind of, don Fernando, but they're not actual photographs... I mean, they are not a photograph you can hold in your hand. I mean, you can't take a photograph of a bitcoin, right? because it only exists as a series of numbers inside a computer, right? Hector is selling a digital address of where this piece of a bitcoin is located on his computer, so that the buyer can click on that address and confirm that the money is there..."

Don Fernando's frown deepened. "Hector is selling pictures of the inside of his computer?" he asked.

"A digital picture, a digital address..." Dan said, then added, "You know how you can click on a *link* on your computer screen, and that link takes you to another document?"

Don Fernando nodded.

"Well, Hector is selling those links. But they are unique; they are one-of-a-kind links; so the buyer is the only person who has that link."

"So the buyer is the only person who can see this picture?" don Fernando asked.

"Well, um, no... Hector is selling other links to other people who can see the same picture," Dan said.

"It sounds like fraud to me, Dani. I don't get it."

"Wait-wait-wait. I've got it, don Fernando," Dan said all excited. "It's like Hector has a museum, and inside the museum—which is inside his computer—there is a piece of a bitcoin, and Hector is selling tickets to people to come into his museum and see the piece of the bitcoin. And every ticket is unique, and the buyer can come into Hector's computer as often as he wants to see the bitcoin."

Don Fernando nodded his head slowly, but said, "Dani, why would anyone spend money to see a picture of a bitcoin? This doesn't make any sense to me. Can't they just buy their own bitcoin? Then they could look at their own bitcoin all day long."

"Well, don Fernando, the reason they are buying the tickets to Hector's museum is because they believe that the tickets will go up in value. The buyers think that *they* can sell the tickets to *other people* and make a profit."

Don Fernando continued to nod his head slowly. "So... they are... what do you call them?... *ticket scalpers*?"

"Exactly, don Fernando!" Dan exclaimed and leaned forward, pointing his finger in the air.

"But again, Dani, the people who the ticket scalpers are selling to, those people could also buy their own bitcoin, right? Why would someone buy a ticket from a ticket scalper to see a picture of a bitcoin when they could buy their own personal bitcoin?"

Dan sighed and collapsed back in the chair. "Well, they are speculating, don Fernando. The people who are buying Hector's links are speculating that they can sell them for more money later on."

"So, Hector is running a gambling scam," said don Fernando.

"It's not a scam," Dan replied. "It plainly says all over his website that these links have zero value, and that he is selling them for entertainment purposes only. In fact, his website is called 'worthless cryptocurrency dot com.' And the buyers have to sign a contract saying that they know that the links he is selling have no value."

"But, then why are people buying them, Dani?"

"Because people are idiots!!" Dan exclaimed in frustration.

"Ah, *that* I understand, Dani."

Just then, Carlos Wang appeared in the doorway to don Fernando's office.

"You wanted to see me, Capitán?"

"Yes, yes, please, come in, Carlos. Have a seat. Dani was just trying to explain to me what my nephew Hector Gonzalez is doing. Dani says that Hector is selling pictures of bitcoin to people over the internet."

Carlos Wang nodded. "Yes, Capitán, that would be one way to explain it."

"Well, give me another way, Carlos, because I do not understand this."

"Your nephew came up with the idea of selling nonfungible tokens that have no value, Capitán. He has a very clever marketing plan where he advertises the fact that these NFTs have no value as a way of making them valuable."

Don Fernando sighed and shook his head. "What is an NFT, Carlos?"

"An NFT, Capitán, is a nonfungible token. It is a unique digital asset that represents ownership of specific content. Your nephew's NFTs are different from regular NFTs in that while his NFT itself is unique, the *content* of the NFT is not unique, that is, people are buying unique NFTs representing a non-unique digital asset, specifically, a satoshi that Hector owns."

Don Fernando covered his eyes with his hand and continued to shake his head back and forth.

Dan spoke up. "I tried to explain it as people are buying a ticket to museum inside Hector's computer, and the ticket allows them to visit the museum anytime they want to see the satoshi."

"Oh, that is good, don Dan," said Carlos. "Yes, I like that explanation."

Don Fernando uncovered his eyes. "What is a satoshi?" he asked slowly.

"It is a tiny fraction of a bitcoin," Dan said.

"Specifically," Carlos added, "it is one hundred millionth of a bitcoin."

"Is it worth anything?" don Fernando asked.

Dan and Carlos looked at each other. Dan said, "Well, a tiny fraction of a penny, maybe." Carlos nodded his agreement.

"So, Hector has these pennies in his computer," don Fernando said, "and he is selling pictures of them..."

"Well, technically, Capitán, the satoshis are in Hector's cold wallet," Carlos said.

Don Fernando's face twitched. "Why... why is the wallet cold?" he asked.

"That just means that actual satoshis are safe from hackers, that no one can steal them from Hector," Carlos explained. "A cold wallet is a small device that Hector can plug into his computer."

"I thought the coins were in his computer," don Fernando said.

"Well, they are," Carlos replied, "in that the digital address is in his computer, but the actual coins are safe in his cold wallet."

"So, he's selling an... address..." don Fernando said slowly.

Dan and Carlos both nodded yes.

"And how much is he selling them for?" don Fernando asked.

Dan just shrugged. He didn't know.

Carlos said, "I think Hector just raised the price to twenty-five dollars each."

"He is selling pictures of a penny for twenty-five dollars?" don Fernando asked in amazement.

Carlos nodded yes.

"Why would anyone spend twenty-five dollars for a picture of a penny?!" don Fernando asked.

"Well, Capitán, the general public is not that bright," Carlos said.

"Yes, yes, Dani explained that part. That is the *only thing* I understand," don Fernando said.

However, dear Reader, things were about to get interesting, because at the same moment that Carlos Wang and Dan were trying to explain to don Fernando exactly what Hector was doing, the Lukov brothers in Switzerland were finalizing their plans to steal Hector's idea and create a fake website that pretended to sell used bitcoin *futures*.

CHAPTER FIVE

Now, before we go any further, dear Reader, I need to apologize. I should have explained earlier who Carlos Wang is. Technically, Carlos Wang is a police officer. He works at the Villa Rosario police station. But he doesn't wear a police uniform, and he doesn't drive around in patrol car. He is don Fernando's computer expert.

As Carlos's last name implies, his DNA heritage is Chinese. His great-grandfather, and many of his relatives, came to Panama—some voluntarily, some not so voluntarily—in the early 1900's, to work on the Panama canal. About thirty percent of Panamanians have Chinese ancestry, and Carlos is one of them. He was born in Panama, and grew up in Panama; and like our young friend Hector Gonzalez, Carlos showed an early aptitude for computers. So much so, that the FBI recruited him out of the University of Panama to go to the FBI computer training school in Quantico, Virginia. Carlos was well on his way to becoming an FBI agent there, when he got homesick and wanted to return to Panama. So he quit the FBI school and moved back home. Don Fernando met him at a hiring fair, and don Fernando—being a forward-thinking police chief—knew that his police department needed a computer expert, and so don Fernando hired him. And that's who Carlos Wang is. Sorry for any confusion.

So, anyway, as I was saying, while don Fernando, Dan, and Carlos Wang were talking, the Lukov brothers were on the other side of the planet, designing their fake website to sell used bitcoin futures. Their plan was simple and complicated at the same time. The simple part was designing the fake website. This was something the Lukov brothers were good at. They had done it many times before.

They were computer-techno-wizards. They were able to design a very elegant website that looked like stock market futures trading chart, with lots of numbers and moving vectors. And it would represent—minute by minute—the volume of sales and current price of used bitcoin futures. This website had every appearance of being part of the Chicago Mercantile Exchange, or CME, except, of course... that it was completely fake.

Now, to be fair, the Lukov brothers didn't just whip this website up in a day. They had been designing it for months, just waiting for a token like Hector's used bitcoin to come along. And Hector's used bitcoin was an absolute perfect fit for this Lukov brothers scam. You see, there *really is* such a thing as a bitcoin futures market. It is regulated by the U.S. Commodity Futures Trading Commission, or CFTC. People can actually buy contracts to buy or sell bitcoin in the future, without having to actually buy the bitcoins themselves. Stock market speculators like to trade in futures because it allows them to lock in a price, which in the case of a volatile commodity like bitcoin, is desirable. Plus, it allows them to use more leverage, so they can buy a large number of futures contracts with a small investment, which increases their chances of a large profit. But main reason that traders like to trade in bitcoin futures rather than buy the actual bitcoin themselves is that they don't have to set up crypto wallets, or worry about crypto hackers, or even understand what cryptocurrency is. It's just *easier* to buy a futures contract on bitcoin than to buy the actual bitcoin.

Of course, there is *no such thing* as a futures market in *used* bitcoins. The Lukov brothers just made that up. It's important to understand this.

So... the simple part of the Lukov brothers plan was designing the fake website, because they already had ninety percent of that done—they just had to plug in Hector's used bitcoin. The more complicated part of their plan was figuring out how to pump and dump the used bitcoins.

The Lukov brothers' plan was to sell future contracts for Hector's used bitcoins through a fake website. Of course,

Hector would never see a dime of that money. He didn't even know the fake website existed. All that money would be pure profit for the Lukov brothers. But they had to figure out a way to generate some buzz in the industry for Hector's used bitcoin. So, the first thing they did was to create about a hundred fake accounts on Coinbase International—the same trading exchange in Bermuda where Hector sold his used bitcoins. Then, the Lukov brothers had their fake trading accounts start buying and selling Hector's used bitcoins, but they were basically buying and selling the used bitcoins between themselves. Each fake account would buy about several hundred used bitcoins from Hector. Then, each fake account would sell their used bitcoins to one of the other fake accounts, who would then sell the same used bitcoins to another one of the fake accounts. This is call "churning," and what it does is create the appearance that there's a lot of trading going on in the used bitcoin market. Trading analysts and financial reporters get very excited when they see trading activity. They think the market is *trying to tell them something*, as if the market was a crystal ball, as if the market had some type of intelligence. When trading analysts see market activity, they get greedy. They start using phrases like "ground-breaking," "cutting edge," "sea-change", or "game-changing." And they want to be "ahead of the curve" and "get in on the action." It's like when a fisherman sees a lot of other fishermen fishing in the same spot, he thinks that's where the fish are, so he joins them and throws his line into the same waters.

And that's exactly what happened to Hector's used bitcoins. In the week that followed don Fernando's meeting with Dan and Carlos Wang, traders started taking note of the rise in activity in used bitcoins on Coinbase's International Exchange, and so they started investing in Hector's used bitcoins themselves. And then financial reporters noticed that traders were starting to invest, so they started writing about used bitcoins in their blogs, vlogs, and newspaper columns, and then the general public started hearing about it, so they started googling used bitcoins, and that's when the Lukov brothers' fake future website popped up, with it's easy links for investing in used bitcoin futures. And that, dear Reader, is how a financial feeding frenzy starts. Novice investors, wannabe crypto traders, and bored and isolated young men who wanted to get rich quick all fell for the Lukov brothers' fake website and its promise of safe investments and guaranteed returns, and they wanted to get in on the action. Some of them started buying used bitcoins on Hector's website, which added to the feeding frenzy. But more of them—much more, one-hundred-times more—started buying futures in used bitcoins on the Lukov brothers' website because, unlike Hector's website, the Lukov brothers' website *guaranteed* them that they would be rich. Plus, they didn't have to have those technicalities like a crypto wallet or a crypto account, or even understand anything about cryptocurrencies in order to buy from the Lukov brothers.

Hector, of course, was completely ignorant of what was driving the demand for his used bitcoins, but he certainly saw the sales demand on his account. He knew he was selling more and more used bitcoins. So, as Ricardo Mendes had advised him, he started raising the price of his token. And that, in turn, drove more sales, both on the Coinbase International Exchange and on the Lukov brothers' fake futures website. As the sales continued to rise, Hector raised the price again. Within the span of a week, he had raised his asking price for his NNFTs five separate times. Now he was selling his used bitcoins for two hundred dollars each. And the orders kept pouring in. Hector had to hire some of his friends at the Computer Club to help him create more and more NNFTs to place on his website for sale. It was a very, very crazy week for the fifteen-year-old.

But, dear Reader, I am getting ahead of myself. So let me go back to the *day after* Dan's meeting with don Fernando and Carlos Wang. Recall that Dan had promised

Hector that he would stop by the Computer Club the next day, and Dan was the kind of person who kept his promises. And so, the next afternoon, Dan was sitting on one of the concrete benches in the Parque Central outside of the House of Culture waiting for Hector to finish up with his Computer Club. Dan figured it would be a short meeting. He would just thank Hector for explaining his project to him the day before, and he would tell Hector how he had shared this information with don Fernando and how don Fernando was pleased with Hector's efforts.

Dan spotted Hector leaving the House of Culture with some of his friends. Unlike the day before, Dan noticed that Hector was very animated; he was speaking loudly, making large gestures, and he and his friends were smiling and laughing and all talking at once. They all looked very excited. *Ah, to be fifteen again,* Dan thought to himself.

Dan waved at Hector. Hector waved back, said goodbye to his friends, and come over to where Dan was sitting.

"Hello, don Dan," Hector said breathlessly, "It is good to see you."

"How are things going, Hector?" Dan asked.

"They are going very well, don Dan. I am getting lots of hits on my website. Everyone at the Computer Club is very excited. I called don Ricardo at lunchtime, and told him what was happening, and he said it was time to start raising the price of my used bitcoins."

"Oh, good, Hector," Dan said. "Ricardo is a smart lawyer. You should listen to him. Maybe you'll make some money with this project."

"I hope so, don Dan. I told my parents that I wanted to buy a new roof for our house. It will be the rainy season in a few months, and last year we had leaks. The roof is very old."

"That would be a good use for your money, Hector," Dan replied.

"Don Ricardo said he would ask my uncle don Fernando to come with me to the bank tomorrow," Hector said.

"Oh? What for?"

"The bank called me today. They had questions about the deposits into my bank account that are coming out of CIE in Bermuda. I tried to explain it to them over the phone, but they did not understand. They wanted to meet with me and my parents. So, I called don Ricardo, and he suggested that I also take don Fernando—you know, because he is the police chief and all—and that way the bank would understand that what I am doing is legitimate. So, I wanted to ask you if you had talked to my uncle."

"Yes, I did, Hector. As a matter of fact, I met with don Fernando and Carlos Wang yesterday, and Carlos and I explained your whole used bitcoin project to your uncle. Now, you need to appreciate that don Fernando is not a computer expert, so I can't say that he understands *exactly* what you are doing. But he *does* understand that it is completely legal, and he is very happy with your success."

"Oh good, don Dan. Thank you so much. That will make it easier."

Dan nodded, but then he thought for a moment. He wondered *why* the bank would even notice an electronic deposit. If the money was being deposited directly into Hector's account from another bank, how would a person at Hector's bank even see it? It would be happening electronically, automatically.

So, Dan asked Hector, "You say the bank called you? Exactly why did they call you?"

"Well, don Ricardo helped me set up a bank account in Bermuda, and that's where CIE deposits my money in dollars. And then that bank transfers those dollars to my bank account here in Villa Rosario," Hector explained.

"Right," said Dan. "I remember that from yesterday."

"Well, there was a deposit this morning that exceeded the automatic account insurance," Hector said.

"I don't understand. What is the automatic account insurance?"

"The bank only insures my savings account up to twenty thousand dollars. If I want more insurance, I have to pay. So, they called me asking if I wanted more insurance. And then they started to ask me questions about the money transfer. I tried to explain, but the person I was talking to wasn't very bright, and they didn't understand."

"Yes, I know the feeling," Dan said.

"So they asked me to bring my parents to the bank tomorrow. So I called don Ricardo, and he suggested I also take my uncle."

"I see. Yes, that's a good idea, Hector."

Then, almost as an afterthought, Dan asked, "How much was the deposit for today?"

"It was fifty thousand dollars," Hector said.

"Wait, what? *Fifty thousand* dollars?!" Dan exclaimed.

"Yes, don Dan. It is a lot of money, I know. I was very shocked."

Dan looked at Hector in disbelief and then repeated, "Fifty thousand US dollars?!"

Hector bit his lip and nodded as if he had done something wrong.

"From the sale of used bitcoins?! Dan asked.

Hector nodded again.

"Over what time period?"

"That was yesterday's sales results, don Dan."

Dan tried to assimilate Hector's words. "You're telling me that you sold fifty-thousand-dollars-worth of used bitcoins since I talked with you yesterday?! Dan exclaimed.

"Sí, don Dan. I couldn't believe it myself."

Dan leaned his back against the concrete backrest of the bench, folded his arms, and just let this fact sink in.

Finally, he said, "Yes... yes, you definitely need to have don Fernando go with you to the bank tomorrow."

CHAPTER SIX

Well, needless to say, dear Reader, Hector's sudden wealth created quite the stir in his family, and among his friends who knew about it. Fifty thousand dollars is not a lot of money to the average millionaire in the United States. But to Hector and his family, it was a vast sum, more than Hector's father would ever earn in his lifetime. So, when Hector told Ricardo Mendes about the fifty thousand dollars deposit, Ricardo suddenly started to take Hector's project very seriously. Ricardo immediately called don Fernando and explained it the situation to him. The bank wanted to meet with Hector and his family at ten o'clock the next morning, so Ricardo asked don Fernando to set up a family meeting at the police station the next morning at nine o'clock so that everyone would be on the same page. Don Fernando, in turn, asked Carlos Wang to come to the meeting. He also called Dan and asked him to come.

And so, the next morning, gathered around a large table in the Villa Rosario police station was don Fernando's sister Elena, Elena's husband Phillipe Gonzalez, their son Hector, along with Dan Landes, Carlos Wang, and Ricardo Mendes. Don Fernando sat at the head of the table. Various low-ranking police officers served coffee and small pastries to everyone. There was much small talk, except for Dan, who wasn't used to being up at such an early hour. Finally, don Fernando stood up, thanked everyone for coming, and introduced everyone, saving the introduction of Ricardo for last. Mostly for Phillipe and Elena Gonzalez's benefit, don Fernando explained that Ricardo was a retired US lawyer, long-time resident of Villa Rosario, and trusted friend. Then don Fernando turned the meeting over to Ricardo. Ricardo thanked don Fernando, and then said the following:

"I want to talk about the big picture here. Most new businesses do not survive. We see that all the time here in Villa Rosario. Small cafes or empanada shops open and then close two months later all the time. And the reasons are always the same: the owners underestimate the start-up costs, or how long it takes for business to get going; or they don't anticipate cash-flow problems or inventory problems; or there is too much competition; or there is simply a lack of demand for their product or service. And those statistics are worse—much worse—for new technology companies, especially in the new crypto-technology field.

"So, when Hector first came to me with his idea for used bitcoins, I thought it was creative; I thought it was innovative; but I wasn't sure how it would actually do in the vast competitive market of crypto tokens. There are over two thousand different cryptocurrencies in existence, and thousands more tokens and NFTs... and 99% of them will not survive. But Hector's idea was really well-thought-out, and—to me—it showed that he had a great future as a businessman or a lawyer. And so, because I thought it would be educational to Hector, I helped him set up various legal entities and bank accounts, mostly really as a teaching exercise. I thought his used bitcoin tokens *might* generate some traction in the crypto-world, but I never thought it would generate this much money. Yesterday, his bank account at Banco Nacional here in Villa Rosario received a deposit of fifty thousand dollars from the sale of Hector's tokens. Banco Nacional was rightly concerned, as this was a large deposit. They called Hector, and Hector called me, and here we are."

Ricardo paused then said. "This morning, however, the bank received another deposit. This one was for seventy-five thousand dollars!"

The people around the table looked visibly shocked. Elena grabbed her husband's hand. Everyone looked at Hector, who just shrugged.

"It's a lot of money," Ricardo continued, "and we all need to go to the bank this morning, and explain to them exactly what is going on. They need to understand that this account is completely legitimate, and that sudden deposits of this nature are normal in the volatile new crypto economy we live in. And so, we will all go down to the bank and reassure them this morning.

"But... the real reason for this meeting is something different. As I said, we have to keep our focus on the bigger picture. The market for crypto tokens is *extremely volatile...* and what does that mean exactly? It means that this money, this sudden influx of deposits, can, *and will*, stop in a heartbeat. That is the nature of fads. With all due respect to Hector, crypto tokens are a fad. At some point, this income will turn off suddenly—come to a complete stop. And so... what is the bigger picture? The bigger picture—and the reason I asked don Fernando to call this meeting—is that we need to protect Hector. New wealth always brings three great risks. The first risk is that people assume the income will continue forever. I guarantee you that is not true. These deposits could stop this afternoon or tomorrow or next week, but they *will* stop. People always assume that the money will flow forever, but that is never the case. I see that Hector already has new shoes and new clothes. That's great. He should be able to celebrate a little. But the bigger picture is that we need to protect his money and save it for his future. In two years, he'll be ready to enter the university, and universities cost money, and I guarantee you that by that time, this sudden inflow of money will be just a memory. This money needs to be protected and invested now, for his future.

"The second risk of new wealth is if people find out about this, it will change how they will treat Hector. Right now, the only people who know exactly how much money has come in are the bank and us here in this room. We must try and keep it that way, although I'm afraid some of the story is going to leak out. When someone comes into money, it's hard to keep it quiet. There's always leakage. Hector's friends at the Computer Club know that sales are booming, and they will tell their friends... and Hector is suddenly going to be treated differently at school. So, we need to think of ways to minimize this. We need to keep the exact total amount of money a secret, if we can. We need to come up with plausible lie that we can tell people, so that they won't start treating Hector differently, asking him for money, and acting like they are his friend when they aren't.

"And that brings me to the third risk of new wealth, which is... bad people. If it gets out exactly how much money Hector actually has, he is at great risk of being kidnapped. I'm sorry to be so blunt, but this is Panama, and these things happen. Don Fernando has agreed to have extra policemen in the park outside of the House of Culture in the afternoons when Hector is there. We think he's going to be safe while he's in school during the day, but there's going to be an extra police car patrolling near his house at night. These are temporary measures, but they need to continue until we see how this used bitcoin fad plays out.

"But the most important thing that we here in this room can do is to keep our mouths shut. No more bragging about used bitcoins, no more talking to our neighbors about Hector's success, and... *no more new tennis shoes, Hector!* We need to adopt a party line, a standard response that we say to everyone. Our automatic response to anyone who asks has to be: *the hidden costs have eaten up all the profits.* We can't deny that he's sold some tokens—everyone already knows that! So we have to downplay the profit. When the neighbors ask how Hector's doing, we need to turn our response into a complaint rather than bragging. We need to say, 'Oh he's sold some of his tokens, but all the profit got eaten up in the fees that the crypto exchange charged him.'

"This afternoon, Hector and his parents and I are going to drive into Panama City and open up a new account for him at Banco General. Then Hector and I will arrange with the Bank of Bermuda to make any future deposits into the Banco General in Panama City instead of Banco Nacional here in Villa Rosario. Hector's deposits will have more anonymity in Panama City than they will here. We don't need any gossipy bank tellers here in town telling their friends about Hector's new wealth. At the Banco General in

Panama City, we can move Hector's money into some CD investments, so they can grow for his future.

"Anyway, that's the big picture. We need to protect Hector; we need to downplay his success; we need to avoid any appearance of new wealth; we need to be alert to the risk of kidnapping. Any questions so far?"

Hector raised his hand. "At the computer club, we've been tracking the daily sales of the used bitcoins. Every there knows how many we've sold as of yesterday. This afternoon they'll see the today's sales."

"Is there any way you can make up some fake charts?" Ricardo asked, "Maybe some charts that show declining sales?"

"I could, but my friends will see the trades on the Coinbase exchange. Coinbase shows both trades and new sales. They can all go to their computers at home and see the current sales figures for used bitcoin."

"Well," said Ricardo, "that's the kind of leakage I was talking about. You will have to ask your closest friends to downplay this information. Be honest with them. Tell them your parents are worried about kidnapping, about strangers asking them for money. Ask your friends to help you keep this information quiet."

Ricardo paused again, then said, "The bright side of leakage is that when used bitcoin prices start to fall, your friends will see that too. Then, they can talk about how fast the sales have dropped all they want."

Dan looked up from his coffee cup and asked, "What about the newspapers? You don't want any stories about 'local boy finds success' or anything like that."

"That's a good point," Ricardo said and looked at don Fernando.

"I will talk to the newspapers," don Fernando said. "They will not print such a story."

Dan nodded. He knew don Fernando's influence. Everyone in town either owed him a favor or wanted to owe him a favor.

Hector raised his hand again. "What about the new roof that I promised my parents?"

"There will be time for that," Ricardo replied. "We still have several months before the rains come. But right now, we don't want to exhibit any evidence of new money. Let's let things quiet down, and then you can get a new roof."

Dan took a sip from his coffee and reflected on the old adage that every problem is a solution to a previous problem. Hector's parents were poor. They did need a new roof. Now they could afford a new roof, but the price they had to pay was the possibility of their son being kidnapped.

Hector raised his hand a third time and asked, "What about raising the price again, I mean, since the token is doing so well?"

Ricardo took a deep breath and thought for a moment. "Well, this is a delicate balance. The purpose of this meeting was to talk about managing the risks of all this new wealth. But you need to make money while you can. You're going to have to monitor the trading figure on Coinbase minute by minute. But given this morning's figures, I think you could raise the price of each used bitcoin to five hundred dollars each. Try and match the trading volume. So, if the trading volume doubles by this afternoon, then double your price."

The room was quiet while everyone started doing math inside their heads. The prospect of Hector's wealth increasing exponentially began to dawn on them.

Meanwhile, over five thousand miles away, in Zug, Switzerland, the Lukov brothers were also looking at most recent trading figures of used bitcoins on Coinbase's International Exchange platform. They were comparing those figures with the sales of the used bitcoin *futures* that *they were selling* on their own website. Hector's tokens were selling well, but the Lukov brothers' futures were selling even better. The futures market, being unregulated, is a shadowy world. Unlike Hector's tokens, whose sales were visible to anyone who had a Coinbase account, only the Lukov brothers knew how much money their fraudulent used bitcoin futures were raking in. As long as Hector's used bitcoin sales went up, the sale of the Lukov brothers' futures would also continue to climb. But the Lukov brothers knew this surge in used bitcoin popularity wouldn't last.

One of the brothers, the one named Georgi, said, "I think we have maybe another twenty-four hours to pump this token up, maybe a thirty-hour window at best. Then we will need to cash out."

The other brother nodded. "How much more money should we put in?"

Georgi replied, "I think two million now, then maybe another two million in twelve hours. Then wait a few hours and see how it does. The faster it shoots up after the second infusion, the sooner we will need to cash out."

The other brother nodded his agreement and said, "Let's do it."

CHAPTER SEVEN

Dan got the news the next morning. He had just gotten up and was pouring himself some coffee when Ricardo called.

"Hey, Ricardo, what's going on?"

"I just got back from the hospital."

"What happened? Are you okay?"

"I'm fine. I was with Hector. His parents and I had to take him to the ER."

"Why?"

"He had a panic attack," Ricardo explained. "He was having trouble breathing. His parents called me, and I insisted he go to the hospital. I took him to the Solano Hospital in La Chorrera. They gave him some tranquilizers to calm him down. He's okay now."

"Wow," said Dan. "He's pretty young for panic attacks. Has this happened before to him?"

"Nope. First time. But it was understandable. Yesterday, we went to Panama City and opened a bank account for him at Banco General..."

"Right, I remember you saying you were going to do that," Dan said.

"Yes, and this morning, that account received a deposit from the Bank of Bermuda..."

"Yeah?"

"And that deposit was for over two million dollars," Ricardo said.

Dan put down his coffee cup. "You're shitting me!"

"No, I'm not. Hector was at home looking at his account online when he saw the deposit and started hyperventilating."

"Wow," was all Dan could say.

"Anyway, I'm calling because I'm trying to set up another meeting with Hector and his family at the police station, for today around one o'clock. Can you make it?"

"Sure, I'll be there."

But, dear Reader, that one o'clock meeting did not happen. Because precisely at noon, which is six p.m. in Zug, Switzerland, the Lukov brothers dumped all their used bitcoins on the Coinbase International Exchange. Now, you'd think that a sudden increase in supply of a commodity would cause prices to fall—you know... how supply and demand is *supposed* to work—but that's not what happens in the ultra-fast lightspeed world of cryptocurrency. What happens in a pump-and-dump scheme is that when the bad guys—which in this case are the Lukov brothers—when they dump whatever commodity they've been inflating, it creates another buying surge in the market; it stimulates more trading, which creates another surge in prices. So, for a brief moment—forty-five minutes to be exact—the price of used bitcoin on the Coinbase International Exchange began to soar again. That's when, inevitably, some blogger or financial influencer will notice this buzz and start thinking critically about it and post the question: *What is the real value of this commodity?* They might raise serious questions about whether this is a hoax, or a rug-pull, or a pump-and-dump, and then that post will go viral and suddenly people will panic and start to sell their shares, or in this case, their used bitcoins. Then the market for used bitcoins will start to falter, and then quickly go into a tailspin and then plunge to zero. The art of a successful rug-pull is timing: knowing the exact moment to sell all your shares before some savvy blogger starts raising questions. And that art was something that the Lukov brothers were very good at.

And that's exactly what happened. The Lukov brothers dumped their used bitcoins, and a feeding frenzy started. Then, some blogger who wrote for the Wall Street Journal posted an opinion piece on the usual social media platforms. That opinion piece was short, because people's attention spans are short, but it was well-written, and it pointed out the obvious fatal flaw in Hector's used bitcoin, which was that it was neither a currency nor a commodity. Nor was it an NFT nor art of any kind, and certainly not something to invest in or even speculate on. In fact, the article suggested that used bitcoin was a fraud, and ended by asking who was behind this token and how much money was he making.

Now, of course, the only money Hector was making was from his sale of *brand-new* used bitcoins, the ones that he was creating and placing on Coinbase to sell. Unlike the speculators who were crowding into the market with buying *and* selling, Hector only *sold* used bitcoins; he never bought them. He didn't have to buy them, because he was making them for free on his computer. When the market went up, that represented what *other people* were selling to each other, and Hector didn't make a dime off that. He made his two million dollars from the new used bitcoin that he had offered for sale the day before. But the Lukov brothers, well... they cleared almost five million dollars from their well-timed sale of all their used bitcoins. And more importantly, they cleared an additional ten million dollars from the sale of their fake futures in used bitcoins. By one o'clock Panama time, which was seven p.m. Swiss time, the market for used bitcoin was worthless, and the Lukov brothers had completely shut down their fake futures website. It simply did not exist on the internet anymore. By eight p.m. Swiss time, the Lukov brothers were counting their profits and high-fiving each other, and Hector was back in the hospital receiving another shot of tranquilizers.

It wasn't until the following day, when the harsh reality had set in that Hector's used bitcoin project was dead, that Ricardo finally got to have his meeting at the police station with don Fernando, Dan, Hector, and Hector's parents.

At that meeting, Ricardo was kind enough not to say, "I told you so." Instead, he focused on the positive: that Hector's project had netted him over two million dollars, and that

Banco General in Panama City was helping them place that money into certificates of deposit that would not only pay for Hector's university, but guarantee a comfortable future for the entire Gonzalez family. Ricardo reminded them that they had been extremely lucky; that the successful survival of a cryptocurrency run was like winning the lottery—it only happens once in a lifetime—and they should thank God for this blessing and focus on building their future.

But you know, dear Reader, how life really works. There's a reason that God was forced to list *Thou shall not covet* as one of his ten commandments. It's because human beings are no damn good. No good deed goes unpunished, and no sudden wealth comes without creating envy. And so it was that while Hector and his family were thanking God for their newfound wealth, that other people were already thinking about how to get their hands on that money.

CHAPTER EIGHT

The first thing that I want to clear up is that there were no legal consequences for Hector's used bitcoin project. I mean, there were clearly consequences—as we shall see—but Hector wasn't prosecutable under any criminal law of any country. And that was because he hadn't done anything illegal. That was the brilliance of the project. Hector had simply created a website called Worthless Cryptocurrency, where he created a thing that was worthless, and he clearly told everyone it was worthless, and he offered that worthless thing for sale, and people bought it. The amazing thing was that people bought it, but of course, people are stupid. You don't need me to tell you that. You only need to look at history. Or even myths. Go back to the story of Adam and Eve. Everyone thinks that story is the story of creation, but it's really the story of how stupidity started. Adam and Eve did the one thing that God told them not to do. Pretty stupid, eh? But the thing that no one ever notices about that story is how Adam and Eve got kicked out of Eden for being stupid, but the snake that seduced them got to stay.

But I digress. I was saying that Hector wasn't subject to any prosecutable criminal liability. That's not to say that there wasn't an outcry for it. Once the news media picked up the story of the rapid rise and fall of used bitcoin, the outrage machine of social media kicked in, and everyone was demanding that someone be held accountable. Bloggers and vloggers and YouTube content creators all jumped on the bandwagon, demanding that heads should roll. For about a month, the internet bandwidth was full of talking heads, claiming that poor working blokes and single moms and people in trailer parks had lost thousands of dollars by speculating on used bitcoins. But these articles all failed to point out two things: first, how utterly foolish those people were; and second, how most of them had lost their money not on Hector's used bitcoins but on the Lukov brother bitcoin futures scam. All the content creators conflated the two, making it seem like used bitcoins and used bitcoin futures were the same thing.

But of course, they weren't the same thing. The investigators at the Office of Foreign Asset Control in the US Treasury figured that out pretty quick. One was clearly based in Panama, and the other appeared to emanate from somewhere in Europe. Those investigators took one look at Hector's website and realized that there was nothing illegal there. And when they dug up screenshots of the Lukov brother's website in the internet archives and saw the promise of guaranteed returns, they recognized the signature style of the two brothers. The US Treasury already had a thick file on the Lukov brothers. But there was nothing they could do. Most overseas internet fraud is beyond the reach of prosecutors. The snake got to stay in Eden, and the Lukov brothers got to stay in Europe.

And so, after about a month, the used bitcoin story simply faded away. Ricardo had done such a good job of stacking the anonymous corporate layers of LLCs and offshore banks, that the mainstream news media never did figure out that a fifteen-year-old boy was the genius behind used bitcoins. And without a villain for the finger-waggers to point a finger at, the outcry for justice evaporated.

However, it didn't evaporate completely. A certain YouTube vlogger named Jerry Armen, who ran a channel called "The Armenian," persisted in the outcry for justice. Jerry was one of those vloggers who liked to yell and scream in his videos, and rage against government. He would either rage against the government for *doing* something, or rage against the government for *not doing* something. No matter what the event, the government was always at fault. It was a technique that obscured his lack of content but enthralled his viewers, most of whom were young men with authority issues.

Jerry liked to post new videos every day. That's how he made his money. The more videos he posted, the more *likes* he got, and the more money YouTube paid him, so that YouTube could post more ads before, during, and after Jerry's videos, which is how YouTube makes its money. And because Jerry posted new videos every day, Jerry made a decent income from YouTube. But that also meant that Jerry needed something to scream about every day. On slow days, he would rail against the government for doing nothing about the used bitcoin collapse, which Jerry called the crime of the decade. It wasn't really the crime of the decade, of course, but facts never got in Jerry's way. He'd start his little video camera rolling in his basement studio, and start ranting and raving about the used bitcoin scandal—how it had destroyed the pensions of little old ladies, and how the government wasn't doing anything about it, which meant that the government must have been somehow behind the scandal.

Jerry had a way of making issues *personal*, almost as if he had lost money on used bitcoin himself. Which, in fact, he had. A lot of money. So, let me give you the background of how Jerry had managed to lose money and why he decided to come to Panama and hunt for the creator of used bitcoin.

You see, Jerry, like a lot of cryptocurrency enthusiasts, had a bit of a gambling problem. And like most gamblers, he was not content with making an investment and waiting for it to mature. He was much more interested in the thrill of the fast buck. So, he didn't buy cryptocurrency; he didn't even buy cryptocurrency futures; he bought cryptocurrency *derivatives*. In other words, Jerry liked simply betting on whether a particular cryptocurrency would go up or down on the market. And where can a person do such a thing? On Polymarket.

Polymarket is an internet trading platform where people can trade cryptocurrency, or cryptocurrency futures, or cryptocurrency derivatives. As the name implies, you can bet on anything on Polymarket. You can bet on the weather or on the outcome of Presidential elections. Polymarket was banned in the US in 2022 by the Commodity Futures Trading Commission, which accused it of running an unregistered derivatives-trading platform. But Jerry, like millions of other Americans, knew how to use a VPN. So, he could access Polymarket and bet all the money he wanted. Polymarket worked by connecting clients to other trading platforms. In fact, Hector's worthlesscryptocurrency.com website was accessible on Polymarket, and so was the Lukov brothers' fake used bitcoin futures website. That was Polymarket's strength—no matter what you wanted to buy, invest in, or bet on, Polymarket could connect you to the appropriate platform to make your deal.

So anyway, Jerry had this YouTube channel, and he fancied himself as a cryptocurrency influencer, on the same level as vlogger Gloria María Hernández in Los Angeles or Roger Van Kette in Florida. But he wasn't as good as them. Although he did have energy along with certain technological skills, he was nowhere near their level in followers or income. He wasn't cute as Gloria and he didn't have the Christian followers that Roger had. But as I said, Jerry was making decent money on YouTube, and, as I also mentioned, he had a gambling problem.

Now, Jerry liked to keep up with his idols, so he watched Gloria's and Roger's channels all the time. In fact, Jerry first heard about used bitcoin from one of Gloria's videos, and so Jerry went to Polymarket to check it out. And that's where he saw the Lukov brothers' futures platform. But Jerry didn't buy Hector's used bitcoins, and he didn't buy the Lukov brothers used bitcoin futures. Why? Because Jerry preferred to trade on Laissez. The Laissez platform—from the French word laissez-faire, meaning *let it ride*—was one of many platforms connected to Polymarket that allowed clients to make derivative bets. In other words, Jerry could go to the Laissez platform and simply bet on whether used bitcoins would go up or down in value. Which is what Jerry did. But the reason that Jerry preferred to do his betting on

Laissez is because Laissez *allowed leverage*—that is, Laissez would *lend you cryptocurrency* to make your bets. In fact, Laissez would lend you *one hundred times* the amount of your bet.

So, long story short, Jerry fancied himself a crypto expert, which he wasn't; and Jerry fancied himself a smart gambler, which he wasn't; and Laissez allowed leveraged bets... so it was the perfect storm. Jerry made some significantly leveraged bets on the Laissez platform that Hector's used bitcoins would go up in value... and he guessed wrong. Actually, it was even worse than him guessing wrong. Because what happened was that Jerry had made his bets just as used bitcoins began to take off, and every hour that used bitcoins continued to rise in value, Jerry would use his supposed profit on Laissez as collateral to make another leveraged bet, which increased his actual leverage to five hundred times his original bet. If Jerry had cashed out his bet at the exact moment that the Lukov brothers dumped their used bitcoins, Jerry would have been a millionaire. But he didn't. And when used bitcoin crashed, so did Jerry's leveraged bets. He woke up one horrible morning owing Laissez one million dollars.

And that, dear Reader, was a very bad situation. Because Laissez, like any illegal leverage gambling company, didn't feel compelled to follow legal methods for collecting their debts. No, no, dear Reader. Like all bookies, money lenders, loan sharks, illegal casinos, gambling dens, and dice joints, Laissez had ways of... shall we say? *communicating* with clients that owed them money. Even though Laissez was illegal in the United States, that didn't stop a group of thugs from showing up at Jerry's condo one day, and forcing Jerry to sign his condo over to them, and informing Jerry that regular payments had to be made to Laissez for the rest of his debt, or else Jerry would lose the ability to use his arms and legs.

And that, dear Reader, is why Jerry had a vendetta against used bitcoin. He didn't blame the Lukov brothers because he hadn't bet on used bitcoin *futures*. He blamed whoever owned Worthless Cryptocurrency LLC, because he had bet on Hector's used bitcoin. Like people everywhere, Jerry was incapable of holding himself accountable for his actions. Someone else had to take the blame. Someone else had to be punished. And that's what began Jerry's quest to track down Hector.

Of course, it didn't take Jerry long to notice that Hector's Worthless Cryptocurrency LLC was a Panamanian company, because it said so right in the legal disclaimer on Hector's website. So Jerry correctly assumed that the corporation would have to have a registered agent in Panama. A registered agent is simply the official person to contact in case of lawsuits. And while the Panamanian government does not disclose the names of directors or shareholders of a registered company, they do keep a list of registered agents, in what is known as the Panama Registry. So, Jerry contacted the Panama Registry and learned that the registered agent for Worthless Cryptocurrency LLC was one Ricardo Mendes, with an address in Villa Rosario, Panama. Now, Jerry could have assumed that Ricardo was just a random Panamanian proxy, but Jerry happened to do a Facebook search and found one Ricardo Mendes, who was a lawyer out of New York, who had retired to Panama. In fact, according to Ricardo's Facebook page, he lived in Villa Rosario. And that, dear Reader, is how Jerry decided to go to Villa Rosario.

CHAPTER NINE

Two months had passed since used bitcoin had burst on the scene, flared up, and burned out. With Ricardo's assistance, Hector used some of his money to buy himself and his parents a new home in the city of La Chorrera, about ten miles northwest of Villa Rosario. This allowed Hector to switch his high school in an effort to leave his notoriety behind him. The sale of used bitcoins went to zero, and Hector and Carlos Wang temporarily closed down the Worthless Cryptocurrency website. Ricardo created a trust corporation to help manage Hector's money. And life slowly returned to normal in the quiet town of Villa Rosario.

And what passes for normal in the country of Panama is, to a very large extent, influenced by the weather. People arise early in the day and try to get all their shopping chores done while it is still cool. The hot afternoons are reserved for siestas, or at least staying out of the overheated streets. The workday resumes late in the afternoon when the heat starts to dissipate, and the workday continues late into the evening. Unless, of course, you are a gringo, in which case the cool evening signals the start of the drinking hour.

And thus it was that on this particular evening, just as the sun was setting, Dan Landes was sitting with Ricardo Mendes in El Balcón, a large bar in the center of Villa Rosario. El Balcón was probably the nicest bar in Villa Rosario, which is not saying much. But it did attract a regular crowd of Panamanians and gringos; and the prices were high enough to keep out cheap drunks and riffraff; and it had a nice view at sunset, and so it was a pleasant place to sit and drink.

Now, when I say it attracted a regular crowd of Panamanians and gringos, that is not to suggest that there were a lot of gringos in Villa Rosario. Gringos occasionally stopped in town, as Villa Rosario was next to the Pan-American highway that connected Panama City to Costa Rica, so it did attract tourists who happened to be driving by around the lunch or dinner hour and were feeling hungry. But Villa Rosario was a small town, and lacked any hotels, so tourists who were passing through never stayed the night. So, the gringos who frequented El Balcón were mostly those few renegades, like Ricardo and Dan, who had actually settled in or around town years ago.

And maybe that's why Ricardo noticed the gringo who was sitting by himself over in the corner of the bar on this particular evening. This guy wasn't a regular, but he looked familiar.

"You see that guy sitting over there?" Ricardo said to Dan.

Dan glanced over to the corner. "Uh huh."

"Have you ever seen him before?" Ricardo asked.

"Nope. Why?"

"No reason. I was just wondering if he was new in town. I saw him this morning as I left my apartment," Ricardo said.

"Probably just lost," Dan said.

"Oh, look! ," Ricardo said. "Catalina is going to hit on him. Let's see what happens."

Catalina was one of the local hookers who hung around El Balcón. The owners permitted them to ply their trade there as long as they weren't too aggressive. Like most bars in Panama, the owners found that having one or two discrete prostitutes in the bar was generally good for business. They would chat up customers, and the customers would buy them drinks, and that kept the bar happy.

Catalina walked up to the gringo stranger, smiled and said something, but the gringo just waved her away.

"Interesting," said Dan. "Most men would have at least chatted with her."

"Maybe he's waiting for his wife," Ricardo suggested.

Something in Dan's old, retired detective brain clicked on. "He's not wearing a wedding ring."

"Your eyes are better than mine," Ricardo said.

Just then, don Fernando entered the bar. While Ricardo and Dan were regulars, don Fernando would only pop in occasionally after work. Don Fernando glanced around the room, spotted Dan and Ricardo, and made his way over to their table.

"Ah, don Fernando," Dan said. "How's the crime business?"

"Crime is up, Dani. Crime is always up," don Fernando said as he sat down. The waiter appeared instantly at don Fernando's side, holding a tray with don Fernando's favorite drink—whiskey over ice. Don Fernando never had to order when he came to El Balcón. The waiters knew what he drank and would immediately bring it to him.

Don Fernando took his drink off the tray, nodded thanks to the waiter, and continued talking to Dan and Ricardo. "Today, we had to arrest some teenagers who were trying to break into houses up in Villa Carmen. They were not local boys. They were from Panama City, driving down here looking for easy targets. We took them back to the station and had a little chat with them. They will not come back to this area."

Dan knew what don Fernando meant when he said he *had a little chat* with those boys. "Villa Carmen? Isn't that a bit outside your jurisdiction?" Dan asked.

Don Fernando shrugged. "It's close enough. You have to stamp these little fires out before they spread. Villa Carmen doesn't have a police department, so we help that village out. Some neighbor spotted those boys driving around slowly, checking out houses. They were not local, so the neighbor called us. By the time we got there, the boys were inside someone's house. We caught them red-handed."

"Speaking of not local," Ricardo said, "do you recognize that gringo sitting over in the corner?"

"I saw him when I came in," don Fernando said, "but I do not recognize him. Why?"

"No reason, Ricardo said. "I saw him near my apartment earlier today. I hadn't seen him in town before, and I was just curious."

"Maybe he's another gringo who wants to move here," don Fernando suggested.

"Yeah," said Ricardo, "except that's he's not at all friendly. Most new gringo light up when they see another gringo. You know—someone to talk English with."

Of course, dear Reader, you know exactly who this stranger was—it was Jerry Armen. As mentioned, Jerry had used his internet skills to track down Ricardo to the town of Villa Rosario. And that really wasn't all that difficult. Ricardo had applied his legal abilities to hide *Hector's* identity, but Ricardo's name was plastered all over the corporate layers of the Worthless Cryptocurrency LLC, and the Coinbase International account, and the bank account in Bermuda. It never occurred to Ricardo to hide *his own* identity. And so it was that Jerry Armen, in trying to discover who was the mastermind behind used bitcoin, kept running across Ricardo's name. And you know how they say that a little bit of knowledge is a dangerous thing? And how they say you can't fix stupid? Well, that describes Jerry: he was a stupid man with a little bit of techno-internet knowledge. He had managed to peel back a few of the corporate legal layers that Ricardo had used to hide Hector's identity. And in doing so, Jerry had come to the completely erroneous conclusion that Ricardo Mendes was the mastermind behind used bitcoin.

Jerry thought he was the only person in the world smart enough to figure out who created used bitcoin. In one sense, he was right: he certainly was the only one in the world who believed that Ricardo was that person. So now, having made this investigative breakthrough, Jerry just had to figure out how to exact his revenge on Ricardo and get his million dollars back.

And in Jerry's overactive but primitive brain stem, there was only one obvious solution to his problem: he needed to kidnap Ricardo. You see, that's the thing about stupid people. Even though they may be very competent in one area—like the way Jerry was very internet-savvy—they are completely incompetent in other areas, like being able to test assumptions, or visualize probable outcomes. In Jerry's mind, because he believed that Ricardo was the mastermind behind used bitcoin, he assumed that Ricardo must own tons of cryptocurrency, and if that were true, then all Jerry needed to do was to kidnap Ricardo and threaten to kill him unless he turned over his cryptocurrency.

CHAPTER TEN

Now, I have to pause here, dear Reader, to warn you that the story gets rather complicated at this point. That's the problem with stupid people like Jerry—because they always misperceive things, they make life much more complicated than it really is. Which is what happened to Jerry.

You see, he began following Ricardo, trying to figure out the best way to kidnap him. Jerry was convinced that Ricardo must own millions of dollars' worth of cryptocurrency because, as I mentioned, Jerry was stupid. But Jerry had convinced himself that Ricardo somehow *owed* Jerry that cryptocurrency because, *somehow*, Ricardo was responsible for Jerry losing his bets on used bitcoin. I know, I know. It sounds stupid when you say it out loud. But that's true for most complicated conclusions that stupid people come to. Stupid people fabricate complicated and erroneous reasons to explain reality, and then come up with a simple but erroneous plan to deal with that reality. And the stupid plan that Jerry had come up with was to kidnap Ricardo, torture him until Ricardo gave him his cryptocurrency, and then return to the United States and pay off the debt to Laissez. Easy-peasy.

So, Jerry starts following Ricardo, trying to learn his daily habits, trying to figure out the best place to execute this kidnapping. But what baffles Jerry is that Ricardo leads a pretty simple life. He doesn't drive a fancy car. He takes the bus. He doesn't live in a fabulous mansion—he lives in a small apartment. He doesn't dress in fancy clothes—he wears simple clothes that look like they came from Goodwill. When faced with this new information, Jerry's stupid mind comes to the obvious conclusion that Ricardo must have a mansion somewhere else in the world. Jerry figures that

Ricardo only comes to Villa Rosario occasionally, to check up on his used bitcoin business, which for some reason, is based in this dusty Panamanian town, probably for tax reasons. And this realization—that Ricardo must have a mansion somewhere else in the world—panics Jerry, because it means that Ricardo is going to leave Villa Rosario soon and return to his mansion. And Jerry doesn't know where in the world that mansion is. Thus, Jerry decides that he has to act immediately, before Ricardo leaves town.

So, the first problem Jerry has is that he doesn't have much time, because he's convinced himself that Ricardo is going to leave town soon. And the second problem is that Jerry can't get a gun, because Panama has strict gun control laws. So, he can't buy a legal gun, and he doesn't have the street skills to buy an illegal one. So, Jerry goes to a local hardware store and buys a nice machete. He figures that if he can't get a gun, that Ricardo probably doesn't have a gun either, and so a nice shiny machete would work just fine in terms of intimidating Ricardo into turning over all his cryptocurrency.

But the third problem that Jerry has is one that he has completely ignored, which is that while he's been in Panama following Ricardo, he has not been making his payments to Laissez. And that's a problem... that's a huge problem.

You see, dear Reader, the world of organized crime actually works in the same way as regular business. Jerry has a debt to Laissez, but Laissez is located outside of the United States because—remember?—Laissez is banned in the United States. So, Laissez does what any good business does when it has a debt that's owed to it: it *sells that debt*. Laissez is not in the collection business. Laissez is in the gambling business... oh, I'm sorry... Laissez is in the leveraged bitcoin derivative business, and not the collection business. So, Laissez sold Jerry's debt.

Now here's where it gets complicated, dear Reader. Laissez is a financial company, so it mainly does business with, and is connected to, other financial companies. So Laissez has to unload Jerry's debt to another financial company so that the transaction looks legit on paper. But that other financial company has to be an expert in collecting illegal debts... so naturally, Laissez turns to Wall Street. This may come as a bit of a surprise to you, dear Reader, to learn that Wall Street is in bed with the mafia, but it's true. Capitalism is based on debt, and nobody likes to pay their debts. But when the bill comes due, someone has to enforce that debt. Since the beginning of time, lenders have had enforcers, which is why the mafia has existed since the beginning of time. Otherwise, nobody would pay their debts. So, Laissez sold Jerry's debt to the Wall Street firm of Pollock & Malpeso, a brokerage firm with ties to the Bonanno crime family. And Pollock and Malpeso, in turn, sold the debt to Izzy Brothers Capital, a smaller firm controlled by the Genovese crime family. And it was Izzy Brothers Capital who first sent several of its larger employees to Jerry's condo the previous month to force Jerry to sign over the condo to them.

So, while Jerry was purchasing his brand-new machete, planning out how to kidnap Ricardo, a large thug from Izzy Brothers Capital was boarding a plane to Panama on a mission to find Jerry.

That's what makes this story complicated. But I'm getting ahead of myself. Jerry had purchased a large machete, and he had waited a few more days to get familiar with Ricardo's daily habits. Finally he decided that this particular night was the night that he was going to visit Ricardo and get his money. He was just waiting until dark.

And so it came to pass, dear Reader, that on this particular night, while Ricardo was home in his little apartment, Jerry came to his door, his machete concealed under a light jacket, and knocked.

Now, if you have traveled at all, dear Reader, you know that every country has a different culture. Sometimes the culture is visible and obvious, like chopsticks versus forks. Sometimes, the culture is invisible, like whether you open the door to a knock or not. In the United States, if someone came to your home and knocked, it would be commonplace to open the door to see who it was. But, unbeknownst to Jerry, this is not the case in Panama. In Panama, you *never* open the door to a knock unless you know who it is. And the reason for that is because home invasion is a problem in Panama. And thus it was, that when Jerry knocked on Ricardo's door, nothing happened. Ricardo heard the knock, and since he wasn't expecting anyone, he said nothing. This, of course, confused Jerry, because he had seen Ricardo enter his apartment, so he knew he was at home. Ricardo had gotten up and walked to the door and looked through the peephole. And Ricardo saw Jerry and recognized him as the gringo he had seen in El Balcón a few nights' earlier. So Ricardo paused, still saying nothing, to consider the situation.

Jerry knocked again, this time a bit louder.

"Who is it?" Ricardo called out.

Jerry had not anticipated that Ricardo would not simply open the door. He had not anticipated that Ricardo would ask him to identify himself. He started to panic.

"I'm looking for Ricardo Mendes," Jerry said.

"Who are you?" Ricardo asked.

"Are you Ricardo Mendes?" Jerry asked.

"What do you want?" Ricardo said loudly.

Now Jerry was befuddled, and when people are befuddled, they sometimes speak the truth.

"I want to talk about used bitcoin," he said.

Now Ricardo clearly knew he was dealing with someone he didn't want to talk with.

"Go away or I'll call the police!" Ricardo said.

Jerry panicked. He didn't know what to do, but he knew that the last thing he wanted was the police. So, befuddled, panicked, and bewildered, Jerry turned and quickly walked away. His head was racing. He was furious with himself. This was not how things were supposed to go. He had fucked up. He was going to have to come up with another plan. He had planned to get into Ricardo's apartment, but that plan would have to wait.

Now, as mentioned, there are no hotels in Villa Rosario. Jerry was staying in a hotel in La Chorrera, a thirty-minute drive away. So, Jerry had plenty of time to come up with a Plan B while he drove his rental car back to La Chorrera. He decided that he would come back to Villa Rosario the next evening, and simply follow Ricardo home, and then accost him at his door with his machete, force him into his apartment, and make him turn over his cryptocurrency then. It was not a great Plan B, but I don't need to explain again that Jerry was not that bright.

But we all know what happens to the best-laid plans of mice and men, right? Well, the same thing happens to the worst-laid plans. When Jerry arrived at the lobby of his hotel in La Chorrera, he was so wrapped up in his own thoughts that he did not notice the very large man stepping out of a parked car and following him into the hotel. And Jerry did not notice that the large man followed him down the hallway of his hotel to his hotel room. Just as Jerry opened the door to his room with his keycard, the man stepped quickly up behind him and gave him a shove that sent Jerry flying into the room and sprawling onto the floor. The large man stepped inside the room and closed the door behind him.

Now this very large man—his name does not matter. Let's call him Izzy, since he was sent by Izzy Brothers Capital. His job was to communicate a message to Jerry. And this particular Izzy's method of communication involved paying two visits to the debtor. On his first visit, Izzy usually said nothing. He was simply there to deliver a vicious beating, preferably breaking one or two bones in the process. Then, a few days later, after the debtor had had time to let this message sink in, Izzy would pay a second visit, to verbally communicate that if money was not forthcoming, there would be another far more serious beating, perhaps a lethal beating.

And so it was that the very large man did beat Jerry that night. Before Jerry could get up from the floor, Izzy squatted down and stuffed a rag over Jerry's face so Jerry could not scream out, and Izzy beat Jerry very hard. At one point Jerry tried to reach for the machete at his belt, but Izzy grabbed Jerry's arm and broke it at the elbow. After this tremendous beating, the very large man let himself out of the room and walked quietly away, taking Jerry's machete with him.

One of the housekeepers found Jerry on the floor the next morning and called the police and an ambulance.

CHAPTER ELEVEN

The next morning, Dan Landes happened to stop by don Fernando's office for coffee. "Happened to stop by" is a bit of an overstatement. Dan went to don Fernando's office intentionally, three or four mornings each week, because don Fernando had the best coffee and these wonderful pastries. The officers at the police station had learned decades ago that having a pot of good coffee and a tray of fresh pastries in don Fernando's office every morning when he arrived made for a much better working environment for the rest of the day.

"Hola don Fernando," Dan said as he appeared in the doorway.

"Ah, Dani. Come in, come in. I have just made some fresh coffee. Help yourself."

Now the truth was, dear Reader, that don Fernando never made his own coffee. Someone on the police force dutifully prepared the coffee pot each morning with fresh Panamanian coffee. Don Fernando had no idea who actually made the coffee. And yet, every morning that Dan showed up, don Fernando would claim that he had just made the coffee himself. It was a little verbal ritual that Dan and don Fernando shared. And then usually, Dan would ask how crime was in the village.

"How's the crime game, don Fernando?" Dan asked as he poured himself a cup of coffee.

"Crime is up, Dani. Crime is always up," was don Fernando's usual response. But this morning he added more.

"In fact, Dani, this may interest you. Remember that gringo that was sitting in El Balcón by himself last week? The one that Ricardo asked me about? Well, he got attacked in La Chorrera last night. He was beaten pretty badly."

Dan was just about to reach for a pastry when don Fernando said this. Dan's hand froze in mid-air. He turned and said, "Don Fernando, I had a call from Ricardo this morning. That guy showed up at Ricardo's apartment last night! Ricardo refused to open the door to him and the guy left."

"Really? Tell me more."

Dan grabbed a napkin and picked up an apple Danish. "Well, Ricardo told me this morning that last night around six p.m., that guy came knocking at his door. Ricardo said he recognized him through the peephole. The guy said he wanted to talk about used bitcoin. Ricardo thought he must be drunk or crazy, so he wouldn't let him in. When Ricardo threated to call the police, the guy left."

"Interesting," said don Fernando. "I wonder if there's a connection. Koki called me this morning and told me about this guy. He was concerned, you know, because the guy is a gringo, and it's bad for tourism in La Chorrera if gringos get attacked."

Dear Reader, I need to pause here and explain who Koki is. Koki is don Fernando's nephew. His real name is Jorge Manuel. Koki is just a family nickname. But Jorge Manuel is the police chief of La Chorrera. He got the job because his uncle, don Fernando, has a particular amount of clout with the nearby towns and cities around Villa Rosario. Anyway, that's who Koki is. I would have mentioned him earlier, but he hadn't appeared in the story yet.

So anyway, don Fernando was saying, "I asked Koki to send me a copy of this guy's passport, and I recognized him from the other night in El Balcón. Koki is going to the hospital today to talk with this man. And he invited me to come along."

"He's in the hospital?"

"Oh, yes. Whoever beat him broke his arm."

"Wow! In La Chorrera?" Dan asked and shook his head in disbelief.

"Yes, Dani. That's why Koki was so upset. It was a violent crime... and against a gringo, too. That is not good."

"Maybe you could take Ricardo," Dan suggested. "You know, so Ricardo can ask him why he was knocking on his door."

"That is a good idea, Dani. I will call him and ask if he wants to come along."

But it was not a good idea, dear Reader, as I shall explain. But don Fernando thought it was a good idea. So, he called Ricardo and invited him; and Ricardo thought it was a good idea, so he agreed to go. And that's how don Fernando and Ricardo ended up that afternoon in the hospital room in La Chorrera, along with Police Chief Jorge Manuel, talking to one very battered and bruised Jerry Armen. And the reason that this turned out to be such a bad idea is that it just solidified in Jerry's mind the erroneous fact that Ricardo was the creator and owner of used bitcoin.

Let me explain what happened.

Jerry was lying in his hospital bed, racked with pain, his arm in a cast, his face swollen and bandaged, his bruised ribs stabbing him every time he breathed, when in walked Jorge Manuel in his police chief's uniform, don Fernando in his suit, and behind them, Ricardo Mendes. The painkillers that the nurses had given Jerry did very little to ease his pain, but they did hamper what little reasoning power he had left. He heard Jorge Manuel introduce himself as the police chief of La Chorrera, and he heard Jorge Manuel introduce the very large don Fernando as the police chief of Villa Rosario. But in Jerry's drugged state, one very large man is just like any other very large man. And the only thing he could remember about the night before was that it was a very large man who threw him to the ground in his hotel room and beat the living shit out of him. So naturally, Jerry assumed that don Fernando was this man! And then, who was standing silently behind both the police and the man who beat him? It was Ricardo Mendes! This just confirmed to Jerry that Ricardo must have enough money to not only buy the police, but to brazenly walk into his hospital room with the police and his attacker! Jerry just turned his head away and moaned. Were they going to arrest him? Were they going to beat him again? He could only half-hear whatever Jorge Manuel was saying. He didn't want to hear. He just wanted to be left alone. Jorge Manuel was saying something, and then the large attacker said something. Jerry just continued moaning, and tried to block out their questions. But when Ricardo stepped up and asked, "Why did you come to my door last night?" Jerry heard that, and he emitted a loud cry. The nurse came in to check on what was happening. Jerry heard her say to the three men that now was not a good time. Thank God for that nurse. The three men left, and the nurse returned with another shot of painkillers. And Jerry drifted off into a blurred sleep.

And that, dear Reader, is how Jerry came to conclude that Ricardo was responsible to him getting beaten up; and that's why Jerry changed his mind about kidnapping Ricardo, and decided to kill him instead.

CHAPTER TWELVE

In the meantime, completely oblivious to all these events, our young friend Hector had been working on a new project. You know, dear Reader, that's the one thing about suddenly receiving a large amount of money: it frees you up. You become more creative, more ambitious. People say that money doesn't buy happiness, but that's not true. It buys you comfort and time and most importantly, it takes away having to worry about where your next meal is coming from. Before the used bitcoin project, Hector and his family were a typical Panamanian family, and by that I mean, they were dirt poor. They lived on rice and beans. Hector had five brothers and sisters, and before used bitcoin, his family's only income was his father's job as a construction worker. It was a hard life.

But now, thanks to the used bitcoin project and Ricardo's legal guidance, Hector and his family were living in a nice house in La Chorrera. Their diet had improved. His father could retire. Hector and his siblings were enrolled in better schools. The future was bright and happy.

And because of all this, Hector had more free time to be creative. He had time to think up more money-making cryptocurrency projects. Because you see, dear Reader, that's the other thing about suddenly receiving a large amount of money: *you want more*. It's the human condition. Everyone says, "Oh, if I had a million dollars, I'd be happy." But it's not true. If you suddenly inherited a million dollars, after you got over the excitement, your brain would naturally and automatically start scheming about how to turn it into two million dollars—or in Hector's case, how to turn his two million dollars into four million dollars. It's the human condition. When it comes to money, everyone wants more.

And that was one reason that Ricardo had convinced Hector and his family to put the money in a structured trust fund, managed by Banco General in La Chorrera—in order to provide for Hector and his family, but also to preserve that wealth for Hector's old age and his grandchildren.

But I digress. What I was saying was that having found financial success in his used bitcoin project, Hector wanted to repeat that experience. So, he came up with a new cryptocurrency project. He called it *Gente Coin*, from the Spanish word *gente,* which means *people.*

Here's the way he explained it to don Fernando: "You see, uncle, it occurred to me that everyone wants to have their own meme coin. So what I did was…"

"Wait a minute, Hector," interrupted don Fernando, "what is a meme coin?"

"A meme coin, uncle, is a cryptocurrency that is cute, like a picture of a dog. Sometimes they start off as a joke. But then people start to trade them, and they can become valuable."

"Why would someone trade pictures of a dog?" don Fernando asked.

Hector shrugged. "Well, partly because they are cute, uncle. No one knows why a meme coin suddenly becomes popular, but it can happen. And when that happens, people will pay money for them. For example, about a year ago, there was a meme coin called Fishface Coin that suddenly got popular. It started as a joke, you see, but it got popular— and people were paying four or five dollars each for them."

"Really? And what are these Fishface Coins selling for today?"

"Today? Oh, I don't know. I think zero or close to zero. Meme coins get popular and then fade away."

"So, they are kind of like dance crazes, or any other fad?" don Fernando asked.

"Exactly, uncle. The most popular ones seem to involve dogs and cats. You know, cute things like that."

"And how many of these meme coins are there?"

"No one knows, uncle, probably thousands."

"And they are a cryptocurrency?" don Fernando asked.

"Well, they want to be, uncle."

"What I mean, Hector, is: can a person actually buy anything with a meme coin?"

"Not really, uncle. They are just cute. But everyone who creates a meme coin hopes that it will catch on, and maybe become the next bitcoin."

"I see. And will that ever happen?"

"No, uncle, I don't think so. They are silly. But they are still popular."

"Okay, Hector. I think I understand. Go on—tell me about your project."

"Well, uncle, as I was saying, it occurred to me that everyone wants to have their own meme coin. So what I did was I wrote a computer program that anyone can use to create a meme coin in their own image. Say, for example, that you wanted to create a meme coin called José Fernando coin. I could just put your name and whatever picture of you that you wanted into this computer program, and it would create a José Fernando coin, and automatically place it on different cryptocurrency exchange platforms for people to buy and trade. You could have your very own meme coin! And every time someone bought one of the José Fernando coins, you would make money, you see? That's why I call these coins *Gente Coins*. They are the people's coins. Everyone can have their own meme coins, their own personalized money!"

Don Fernando nodded. "I think I understand, Hector. And this is an application that a person can download onto their phone?"

"No, uncle. The program is too large for that. My plan is to reopen my Worthless Cryptocurrency website and offer this new Gente Coin there. People would send me one hundred dollars and I would create the meme coins for them. That would be my sales pitch, you see? The only fee is a one-time, upfront cost of one hundred dollars. I don't take any commission from the sale of their meme coin. They will get to keep all the profits from the sale of their coins."

"And you think people will send you money for this?"

"Oh, yes, uncle. It is very difficult, almost impossible, for the average person to create a meme coin. You have to know a lot about computer programming. And then, you have to create an account on a cryptocurrency exchange platform. Then you have to have accounting software that collects the money and sends it to you. It's very complicated. But that's the beauty of this new project. I make it so simple, so easy, for the average person to create their own cryptocurrency. All they have to do is send me one hundred dollars and a picture of their face and type in a few answers on the computer screen. Everyone will have their own image on their own money. Everyone will be famous!"

"And you think people will buy this?"

"Well, I think gringos will, certainly," Hector said.

"Yes, that is a good point, Hector. Gringos all want to be famous."

"Carlos Wang is helping me put the finishing touches on the computer program. We're going to test a prototype tomorrow. As soon as we've got all the bugs worked out of the program, don Ricardo is going to help me do the legal paperwork, to make sure I'm protected. I think this is going to be a moneymaker, uncle."

And that, dear Reader, is how Hector's new project, his Gente Coin, was created. And about a week later, when Worthless Cryptocurrency, LLC, came back online announcing the launch of Hector's Gente Coin, three important things happened. The first thing was, of course, that the so-called smart people, the people in the know— the fintech financiers, crypto-hipsters and meme coin maniacs—all took notice of the launch, and started sending Hector payments of one hundred dollars each. The second thing that happened was that Jerry, who had been released from the hospital, saw that the Worthless Cryptocurrency website was back online. This further enraged him and made him more determined to murder Ricardo. And the third thing that happened was that the Lukov brothers in Switzerland sat up and took notice.

You see, unlike Jerry, the Lukov brothers had a very favorable attitude towards whomever had created used bitcoins on the Worthless Cryptocurrency website. Used bitcoin had made the Lukov brothers a lot of money. So, when they saw that the Worthless Cryptocurrency website was offering a new coin, they were very interested.

"You know, Georgi," one Lukov brothers said to the other, "this Gente Coin is a clever idea. The brain behind this Worthless Cryptocurrency company is very shrewd. He will make a fortune with this."

"Yes, Dimitar. I've been trying to think of a way we could piggy-back on this idea, but I don't see how. It is too complete of an idea."

"Maybe we should just steal it, Georgi—you know, create a counterfeit Gente Coin."

"Maybe... maybe... but maybe we should just go and talk with this person and see if he wants to work *with* us. This person is obviously very smart and very ambitious. We have several unfinished projects that he could help us with. I think that the three of us could make more money by working together."

"Oh, that is a good idea, Georgi! Yes, I like that idea. I will do some research and see if I can find out who and where he is."

Because you see, dear Reader, what the Lukov brothers were assuming was that whoever was behind used bitcoin and Gente Coin was exactly like them. People always do this, you know. They assume that whomever they are dealing with must have the same motivations, the same emotions, and the same perspective as them. The Lukov brothers didn't know that they were dealing with a fifteen-year-old boy who happened to be a computer nerd, and who happened to like inventing things. They thought they were dealing with some fifty-year-old power-hungry greedy Elon Musk knockoff with no scruples, who had an insatiable appetite for money. In other words, they were projecting who *they were* onto whom they imagined was behind Worthless Currency, LLC. So, of course, they assumed that this person would want to join forces with them, and make even more money. It's a common mistake, this phenomenon of projection. In fact, it happens every second of every day to everyone all the time. When it comes to other people, all perception is made up of thousands of little projections. And it's little mistakes like this that set into motion great events. And it was *this* little mistake that eventually caused the Lukov brothers to travel to Panama.

CHAPTER THIRTEEN

Not all perfect storms are perfect, dear Reader. You might spot a rogue wave, a huge tsunami, on the horizon, and think that it is going to wipe out your coastal village. But then... it peters out before it even gets to the shore. In fact, if you see a perfect storm coming, those are usually the ones that fade away. *Real* perfect storms hit you without warning, and it's only later, *much later*, when you drag your soggy ass to safety and look back on what happened that you can begin to piece together how the elements all fell into place to create the perfect storm.

And so it was that on a certain evening in the little town of Villa Rosario, a perfect storm emerged out of nowhere and swamped the tiny apartment of Ricardo Mendes. Let me describe what happened:

Jerry had been released from the hospital. The first thing he did was move to a different hotel, which was a normal reaction for a person in his position. After all, he had been beaten up horribly in his previous hotel room, so he did not want to return there. Of course, he was under the erroneous perception that it was don Fernando who had attacked him. But that was because his brain had been infused with painkillers in the hospital when don Fernando and his nephew Jorge Manuel and Ricardo had shown up to question him. Nonetheless, he had a fear that don Fernando would return to beat him again. In reality, it was the man I've nicknamed as Izzy who beat up Jerry. I'm just calling him Izzy because he's an enforcer who works for Izzy Brothers Capital, the mafia-connected debt collection service. As you may recall, Izzy Brothers Capital had purchased the debt that Jerry had incurred when he lost his leveraged bet on used bitcoin that he had made on the Laissez platform. I warned you earlier, dear Reader, that things were getting complicated. Anyway, Izzy had temporarily lost track of Jerry after he had beaten Jerry up. He wasn't sure which hospital Jerry had been taken to. And then Jerry switched hotels. So, Izzy was trying to find Jerry again, because he needed to explain to Jerry why he had beaten him, and that he would beat him again if he didn't start making payments on the debt he owed.

In the meantime, don Fernando had obtained some surveillance video from Jerry's old hotel, and it clearly showed Izzy coming into the lobby of the hotel and going down the hallway where Jerry's room was located. Don Fernando took the clearest photo of Izzy from this video and forwarded it to National Migration Service of Panama, which monitors all travelers coming into and out of Panama. And the Migration agency was able to match Izzy's photo with a certain passport of a certain man who had entered Panama recently. So now, don Fernando had Izzy's real name and a copy of his passport. With that he was able to run a background check. And don Fernando did not like what he found. Izzy had multiple arrests over the years in the US for various assault charges. But none of them had resulted in felony convictions, because all the witnesses decided not to testify at the last minute. Izzy was on an FBI watchlist of possible mafia-connected persons, but because he had no felony convictions, he was still able to enter Panama. All this was enough to convince don Fernando that he needed to find Izzy and persuade him to leave Panama as soon as possible.

Also, in the meantime, Hector, Carlos Wang, and Ricardo were fine-tuning Hector's new Gente Coin project. Amazingly enough, money was once again rolling in, and Ricardo was helping Hector funnel that money into a second trust fund for Hector and his family.

Finally, in the meantime, the Lukov brothers had discovered the same thing that Jerry had discovered weeks earlier—that Ricardo Mendes's name was all over the documents that created the Worthless Cryptocurrency accounts on Coinbase in the Bahamas and the LLC in Panama. Unlike Jerry, the Lukov brothers did not automatically assume that Ricardo was the mastermind behind the Worthless Cryptocurrency empire. But they did figure that if he wasn't the creator, he would know who was. And thus it was, dear Reader, that the Lukov brothers decided to fly to Panama.

So, you now see, dear Reader, how this perfect storm was starting to swell up and gain momentum. But here I must—and I apologize for doing this—but I must introduce another person to the story, and that is a certain FBI agent named Brian Rooney. Remember how I explained earlier that the FBI had a thick file on both Georgi and Dimitar Lukov, but they had never been able to touch them because Switzerland has strict privacy laws and is very liberal about cryptocurrency? However, that didn't stop the FBI from keeping tabs on them. So, when the Lukov brothers left Switzerland and flew to Panama, the FBI got very excited. For one thing, Panama and the US have a strong extradition treaty. And even though it's illegal, the FBI also has many agents working *inside* Panama—you know, just to keep an eye on things. So, when the Lukov brothers flew to Panama, the FBI sent agent Brian Rooney down to Panama to find out what was going on.

Through FBI informants who worked at Panama's National Migration Service, agent Brian Rooney learned that when the Lukov brothers had arrived in Panama, they had listed a hotel in the city of La Chorrera as their intended destination. Now, I should explain that the FBI not only keeps files on bad guys—they also keep files on friends and good guys, and thus they had a file on don Fernando. Over the years, don Fernando had written many grant requests to the FBI for money to help in the never-ending battle against drug cartels. Now, truth be told, Villa Rosario did not really have a problem with drug cartels. But the town's police department was able to use the FBI's money for new uniforms and salary increases for its officers. And the quarterly reports that don Fernando sent to the FBI spoke glowingly of their success against the drug trade. Don Fernando's use—or misuse—of FBI grant money is a long story that does not concern us here, but let's just say that the FBI believed don Fernando's reports and viewed him as an ally. And so, when agent Brian Rooney was tapped to go Panama, he was given the file on don Fernando to read, and he was told that when he arrived in La Chorrera he should go to the nearby town of Villa Rosario and speak with don Fernando.

And so it was that one morning, don Fernando received a call from this agent Brian Rooney. It was a very polite call wherein agent Rooney introduced himself, and explained that he had just arrived in Panama, and asked if he could come and talk with don Fernando that very afternoon. Don Fernando was gracious and overwhelmingly polite and said "of course," and the two men agreed on a meeting time of two o'clock.

After the phone call ended, don Fernando immediately called Dan Landes.

"Dani, I got a call from the FBI today! They want to come and talk with me this afternoon!"

"Really? What do they want to talk about?"

"I don't know, Dani. That's what makes me nervous. I sent them statistics last month on all the drug arrests we made."

"Drug arrests? In Villa Rosario? I didn't know about that."

"Yes, Dani, that's what worries me. I'm afraid they will ask what happened to all those criminals."

"Oooh, I see, don Fernando. Well, just tell them that they are all in pretrial detention somewhere in Panama City... No, wait, better yet, tell them that they were all illegal immigrants from Colombia, and that they were deported."

"Ah, yes, Dani. That is a good idea. But, um, I want to ask you... can you come to the meeting this afternoon? You know, just in case I need a *translator*?"

"Of course, don Fernando. What time is the meeting?"

"Two o'clock."

"I'll be there."

"Thank you, Dani."

Now, I should explain, dear Reader, that don Fernando's English was quite good. He didn't need an actual translator. But on those rare occasions when US officials of any capacity came to Villa Rosario, don Fernando would often pretend that his English wasn't that good, and that Dan would translate. That ruse gave don Fernando and Dan time to improvise what to say. It also gave them the excuse of a bad translation in case things went wrong.

And thus it was that on that afternoon don Fernando and Dan Landes welcomed FBI agent Brian Rooney into the conference room at the Villa Rosario police department. Don Fernando explained in broken English that Dan was present just for translation purposes.

"How's your Spanish?" Dan asked Agent Rooney.

"I don't speak a word of Spanish," Agent Rooney replied.

"Well, I'm here to help," Dan said and smiled to himself.

After deputies had served everyone coffee, agent Rooney got down to business.

"Police chief Fernando, the reason for my visit is that the FBI is tracking two brothers from Bulgaria who have recently arrived in Panama, and we need your help. These two brothers are involved with financial fraud."

Agent Rooney opened his briefcase and removed several photos from a file folder and slid them across the table to don Fernando and Dan. Don Fernando breathed a sigh of relief. It appeared that Agent Rooney was not there to talk about fighting drug cartels.

"These are the Lukov brothers, Georgi and Dimitar Lukov. They are twins, and as I say, they are originally from Bulgaria, but they have been living in Switzerland for the past ten years. They've been on our radar for a long time. They are fraudsters, and their current specialty is cryptocurrency fraud. Their latest venture was an internet pump-and-dump scheme involving something called used bitcoin futures."

Both Dan's and don Fernando's ears pricked up when they heard Agent Rooney say the words *used bitcoin*, but they both instinctively kept their faces from showing any kind of reaction.

Brian Rooney continued. "This venture involved selling phony derivative futures contracts on various internet investment platforms. These derivative contracts claimed to be based on an actual token called a used bitcoin, which we believe was a meme coin that was being sold humorously somewhere here in Panama. The actual used bitcoin had no value. But the Lukov brothers used social media to convince gullible investors that the futures contracts that they offered were going to go up in value. These future contracts were completely fake, of course. But in order to create the illusion of value, the Lukov brothers bought thousands of the *actual used bitcoins* on Coinbase, which caused it to go up in value, which in turn caused people to buy the Lukov brothers' future contracts which they had advertised as a safe investment alternative. Then, at the peak, the Lukov brothers sold all their meme coins and got their money back from that. But, by then, thousands of people had purchased used bitcoin *futures contracts* from them which, in fact, were worthless. We estimate that the Lukov brothers swindled investors out of ten million dollars by convincing them to buy these phony future contracts."

Dan held up one finger, indicating he needed Agent Rooney to pause for a moment. Then Dan turned to don Fernando and asked in Spanish, "Do you understand what he is saying, don Fernando? Do you know what a *futures contract* is?"

"I think so, Dani," don Fernando replied in Spanish. "Carlos Wang tried to explain it to me once. It's where you promise to buy or sell something in the future, even though you don't own it today."

"Exactly. So this agent is saying that these two brothers were selling fake futures contracts that were based on Hector's used bitcoin."

"I don't think Hector knew anything about this, Dani."

"No. I don't think so, either. This was something entirely separate."

"So let me see if I understand, Dani. This FBI agent is saying that these two Russians were running an internet scam..."

"Well, they are from Bulgaria, don Fernando, not Russia."

"Bulgaria, Russia, it's all the same Dani. These two Russians were running an internet scam selling phony contracts to buy Hector's used bitcoins, and that *they* are the ones responsible for why the used bitcoins got so popular?"

"It kind of sounds that way, don Fernando. That would explain a lot."

Don Fernando nodded his head.

Dan turned to Agent Rooney and asked, "Just to be clear, these futures contracts that these two Russians were selling..."

"Bulgarians," interjected Agent Rooney.

"Yes, these future contracts that these two Bulgarians were selling had no connection to the actual used bitcoin?"

"Correct," said Agent Rooney. "They were completely separate. This is part of the Lukov brothers' MO. They take a legitimate asset and then create a counterfeit version of it, or some kind of derivative of it, to sell to unwitting investors."

"What is a MO, Dani?" don Fernando asked in Spanish.

"It stands for method of operation. It means their style of crime."

Dan then turned back to Agent Rooney and said, "Police Chief Fernando wants to know how he can help."

"Well, we know that the Lukov brothers have checked into a hotel in the city of La Chorrera. But we don't know *why* they have come to Panama. We have some theories, but we are really in the dark. We were hoping that the Police Chief could use his network of informants to find out why the Lukov brothers are here."

Dan turned back to don Fernando. "You have a network of informants?" he asked in Spanish.

Don Fernando nodded sheepishly. "Yes, well, you know... to fight the drug cartels."

"Ah, yes. I understand," Dan said.

Dan turned back to Agent Rooney. "The police chief said he would be glad to help."

"The other thing we could use help with," Agent Rooney said, "is that we'd like your help in locating an American citizen named Ricardo Mendes. We believe he may be living here in Villa Rosario."

Both Dan and don Fernando kept their faces expressionless at the mention of Ricardo's name, as Agent Rooney continued.

"As I said, we have several theories why the Lukov brothers have come to Panama. And one of those theories is that he is here to meet Ricardo Mendes. We don't think they know each other. We have analyzed all of Lukov brothers' phone calls, emails and texts, and all of Ricardo Mendes's phone calls, emails and texts. And we don't see that they've ever had any correspondence with each other. But we are assuming that there must be *some* connection, because they both were involved in this used bitcoin business."

Don Fernando turned to Dan and said in Spanish, "What do you think, Dani?"

"I don't know, don Fernando. Let me ask."

Turning to Agent Rooney, Dan asked, "This Ricardo Mendes, he's a Panamanian?"

"No, he's a US citizen. But he's retired and living here. Evidently, he was involved in setting up the used bitcoin accounts on Coinbase. But we don't see that he's ever received any money from used bitcoin. That confuses us. Either we've got the wrong guy or he's laundering money through some offshore account we don't know about."

"But you've been monitoring him?" Dan asked. "Reading his emails and tapping his phone?"

"Well... yes. That's what we do. We're the FBI. We keep tabs on people."

Dan nodded. Don Fernando said to Dan in Spanish. "Let it be, Dani. Tell him we will find his Ricardo."

"Don Fernando said he will find out everything about this person," Dan said to Agent Williams. "He wants to know what else he can do to help his friends at the FBI."

"That's about it," agent Rooney said. "We want to know why the Lukov brothers are here and whether it has anything to do with this Ricardo Mendes fellow."

"Tell him he can count on us," don Fernando told Dani.

"Police Chief Fernando says that you can count on him," Dan said.

And with that, the FBI agent said his goodbyes to the smiling police chief and his translator friend and left the police station.

After he was gone, Dan turned to don Fernando and said, "We need to go and warn Ricardo."

CHAPTER FOURTEEN

Meanwhile, as I mentioned earlier, Jerry had been released from the hospital. The hospital had given him a thirty-day supply of pain pills. Jerry, however, didn't have much self-discipline, and his pain from the beating he had received was immense, so he was doubling up on the pain pills. This eased his pain, but it also further clouded his ability to reason. As I also mentioned, he had changed hotels, and as fate would have it, he had selected the very same hotel in La Chorrera that the Lukov brothers had chosen. And so it was, dear Reader, that Jerry happened to meet the Lukov brothers.

Fate is a strange thing. It's almost as if Fate has a twisted sense of humor, the way it plays with us, making it appear as if things are working out a certain way, only waiting to pull the rug out from underneath us at the last minute.

So, what happened was this: that same afternoon, while FBI Agent Rooney was visiting the police station in Villa Rosario, Jerry was scouring the pawn shops in La Chorrera. He was hoping to find a gun, because he had definitely decided he was going to kill Ricardo Mendes. But, as mentioned, illegal guns are very difficult to get in Panama. They are not impossible to find, but it takes more criminal skill and persuasion than Jerry possessed. He thought he might buy another machete, but instead he found a razor-sharp hunting knife at one of the pawn shops, and in his altered mental state, Jerry decided that a hunting knife was better than a gun because it wouldn't create any noise. And it was better than a machete, because it was lighter and easier to conceal. So, he bought it.

Then, later that same afternoon, Jerry went down to the hotel bar in La Chorrera to have a drink to celebrate his new purchase. He had discovered that drinking seemed to enhance the pain pills he was taking. And in fact, the alcohol was doing exactly that, eliminating *all* of Jerry's pain, and making him feel like his old self again. And his old self, as you might imagine of a man who did podcasts and YouTube videos for a living, was a talkative self.

And it was at this hotel bar where Jerry met the Lukov brothers. Now, the Lukov brothers, being Bulgarians, were heavy drinkers. Unlike Jerry, they could hold their liquor. And as they sat there drinking at their table, they noticed Jerry sitting at the bar talking in an animated fashion with the bartender. Their ears pricked up when they heard Jerry using the words "cryptocurrency" and "used bitcoin." How strange, they thought, that sitting in a bar in a small town in Panama, they would hear someone, who was obviously an American, talking loudly about used bitcoin, the very topic that had brought them to Panama. So, they kept their eyes on Jerry, watching him, wondering who he was.

And Jerry, even in his talkative inebriated state, eventually noticed that the Lukov brothers were staring at him. So, he looked back. He had to blink his eyes and shake his head, because—as I mentioned earlier—the Lukov brothers were twins. At first, Jerry thought he was seeing double, and the thought crossed his mind that maybe he ought to slow down on the drinking. But he blinked and looked again, and by God, he was looking at twins! And the Lukov brothers saw that Jerry was staring at them and Jerry saw that the Lukov brothers realized that he was staring at them. So, Jerry did the American thing: he smiled and waved and got off his barstool and stumbled over to the table where the Lukov brothers were sitting.

Now, drinking cultures vary from country to country. In the US, people go to bars to meet other people. So, it's natural—in the States—for someone to go over to a table of strangers and introduce themselves. But this is not the culture where the Lukov brothers came from. In Bulgaria, and to a similar extent, in Switzerland, people go to the bars to drink. So, when Jerry came lurching over to their table, the Lukov brothers were taken aback. One of the brothers slid his hand under his jacket toward his armpit. And the reason that one of the brothers slid his hand under his jacket was because—unlike Jerry—the Lukov brothers were actual criminals. They knew how to get an illegal gun when traveling in a foreign country. The Lukov brothers had gone to the same pawn shops that Jerry had gone to earlier, but when the pawn shop owners claimed they didn't have any pistols for sale, the Lukov brothers just smiled and reached over the counter in a friendly way, grabbed the owner's arm and twisted it in a direction it was not meant to go, and suggested that the owner may have forgotten a small pistol or two that he might actually have in the back, and might be willing to sell them. The Lukov brothers didn't like moving around without being armed. And so it was that when Jerry approached their table, Georgi Lukov instinctively reached toward the pistol strapped under his arm.

But Georgi did not have to pull his gun out. In fact, the guns that the Lukov brothers were carrying in the bar at that moment stayed safely hidden in their holsters. I only mention this to give you an idea of the character of these two brothers. The guns come into play later... but I am getting ahead of myself...

So, Jerry staggered up to the table where the Lukov brothers were sitting. He smiled broadly and said, "You're twins, eh?"

Of course, this was not news to the Lukov brothers, but they smiled politely and nodded, and waited to see what this drunk American wanted.

"I saw you looking at me, and I thought I was seeing double!" Jerry announced.

Dimitar Lukov decided to seize the moment and said, "We heard you talking about used bitcoin."

"Ah yes, used bitcoin," Jerry said. "I'm a bit of an expert in that area, if I don't say so myself. Allow me to introduce myself. I'm Jerry Armen. I run a YouTube channel called *the Armenian*. Perhaps you've heard of it."

Well, dear Reader, imagine the shock in the Lukov brothers at that moment. Because, yes! they had heard of Jerry's channel. They had reviewed all of Jerry's YouTube videos when they were researching how to rip off the whole used bitcoin concept. They thought Jerry's videos were loud and stupid, but they found them useful, and most importantly, they noticed how many "likes" Jerry's videos on used bitcoin had received. Once Jerry said his name, the two brothers each recognized his voice.

The Lukov brothers looked at other in disbelief. How coincidental, they both thought simultaneously. How strange and coincidental that they should run into Jerry Armen in the tiny town of La Chorrera, Panama.

"Please," gestured Georgi Lukov, "sit down. Of course, we've heard of you. We are big fans. Let us buy you a drink."

Jerry, like any American, was delighted to be recognized, and so he sat down. The Lukov brothers signaled the waiter to refill Jerry's glass. Jerry was already pretty hammered, but he was not one to refuse a free drink and an audience.

Georgi took the lead. "Yes, we listen to your podcast, Jerry Armen. Yes, we find it very, um, very good, very informative. Tell me, Jerry. What brings you to Panama? Are you here because of used bitcoin?"

"Exactly," exclaimed Jerry, pointing with his hand and spilling a few drops of his now-full drink. "I'm here because of used bitcoin, that fuck fraud used bitcoin! It was a scam, a total scam!"

"But why here?" asked Georgi. "Why Panama?"

"Because that's its homebase! It's *here*! In the next town over! Villa whatever! That's where they ran the scam!"

Georgi and Dimitar quickly glanced at each other. "*Who* ran the scam?" Georgi asked.

"Ricardo Mendes!" said Jerry as he took a slurp of his drink. "He lives in the next town over."

"You *know* him?" Georgi asked in disbelief.

"Yes! I know him. He has my money!"

Georgi and Dimitar looked at each other again. They couldn't believe their luck.

"Can you introduce us to him?" Georgi asked. "We would like to meet him."

Jerry looked up from his drink. The Lukov brothers, as you might imagine, were rather large fellows, solid Bulgarian stock, thick necks, not what you would call handsome. In Jerry's inebriated mind, he saw himself entering Ricardo's apartment flanked by these two gangster-looking hulks. Yes, he thought, that would make quite an impression on Ricardo Mendes. Maybe that would be enough to frighten Ricardo Mendes into giving him back his money. If not, he would kill Ricardo, and maybe these two would help him.

"I'll take you to his house," Jerry said. "I have some unfinished business with him. In fact, I will take you to him tonight!"

And that, dear Reader, is how alliances are formed. They are always based on opportunity, misunderstood intentions, and miscommunication. The Lukov brothers wanted to meet Ricardo, in order to find out the mastermind behind used bitcoins, so that they could do some business together. And it would be very convenient if Jerry could introduce them to Ricardo. In order to accomplish this, they would overlook Jerry's drunkenness, and ignore whatever business Jerry had with Ricardo. Jerry, on the other hand, wanted his million dollars back—the money he had lost on used bitcoin. And if he couldn't get his money back, he would kill Ricardo. In fact, he planned to kill him regardless. So, Jerry would ignore whatever motivations these two goliath twins had for meeting Ricardo and take them to Ricardo's apartment in order to exact his revenge.

And thus it was, dear Reader, that three men left the hotel bar that night: the drunken Jerry Armen, who had a very sharp hunting knife in a sheath attached to his belt, and the two Lukov brothers, each with a pistol stowed underneath their jackets. They left the bar and hailed a cab to take them to Villa Rosario. But there was also a fourth man, who had been sitting in his rented car outside the hotel. It was Izzy, the man who had attacked and beaten Jerry a few days earlier. He had located Jerry's hotel and had just started surveilling it. He had only been parked outside the hotel for a few minutes when he spotted Jerry leaving the bar with two large men. For a moment, Izzy wondered if the two large men were debt collectors like he was, but then he saw how friendly the three men were acting towards each other. "They're drunk," Izzy thought to himself and smiled. He congratulated himself on his good luck in spotting Jerry. Izzy put his car into gear and began to follow the cab.

CHAPTER FIFTEEN

Dear Reader, before I get to what happened when Jerry and the Lukov brothers arrived at Ricardo's apartment, I need to back up to a few hours earlier, to the mid-afternoon. Recall that FBI agent Brian Rooney had just left don Fernando's office, and that Dan had said to don Fernando, "We need to go and warn Ricardo." Well, that's exactly what don Fernando and Dan did. They got into don Fernando's police car and drove straight over to Ricardo's apartment.

"Ah, Ricardo, I'm glad you are home," Dan exclaimed when Ricardo opened the door. "Can we come in?"

"Of course. What's up, guys?"

"We need to talk," don Fernando explained. "We just left a meeting with an FBI agent, and this FBI agent wants to talk with you."

Well, you can imagine, dear Reader, what effect these words have on anyone, especially an US expat living in another country. There's no sentence quite as nerve-racking as the sentence *the FBI wants to talk with you.*

But on the other hand, Ricardo, as you may recall, was a retired lawyer, so his response to don Fernando was pointed. "Aren't they a little bit out of their jurisdiction?"

"Yes, I guess they are," Dan said, "but they still want to talk with you."

"What about?"

"We're not exactly sure," Dan said, "but it has something to do with used bitcoin."

"This FBI agent called me this morning," don Fernando explained, "so I set up a meeting with him for this afternoon. I invited Dani to be there, you know, just in case. I thought maybe this agent was wanting to talk about drug cartels. The FBI is always interested in fighting the drug cartels. But this fellow shows up, and he does not talk about the drug cartels. He is following these two brothers from Russia…"

"Bulgaria," Dan interjected.

"Wherever," don Fernando continued. "These two brothers are named Lukov. He said they are twins. That is always a bad sign, you know. Twins are the Devil's stepchildren. Anyway, these two Russian twins, evidently they made some kind of scam involving used bitcoins. And they stole millions of dollars from people, including US citizens."

Ricardo listened intently, then said, "I've never heard of these guys. What exactly was their scam?"

"Evidently," explained Dan, "they had a racket, where they were selling used bitcoin *futures* on the internet…"

"Used bitcoin futures?" interrupted Ricardo. "What the fuck are those?"

"Some kind of contract to buy used bitcoin futures," repeated Dan. "It was some type of derivative, based on Hector's used bitcoin."

"Really?! I never saw anything like that on Coinbase," exclaimed Ricardo.

"It was on the black web," don Fernando said.

"Well," said Dan, "I don't know what platform it was on, or whether it was on the dark web or not. This FBI agent didn't give us much detail, but he did say that the way this scam worked is that these two brothers bought *tons* of Hector's used bitcoin to pump the market up, and *that* caused their sale of their derivative contracts to skyrocket, and then they cashed out their used bitcoins when it peaked. So, they profited from Hector's coin, and they kept all the cash from phony futures contracts."

Ricardo's mind was racing. "So, this guy was saying that *these two brothers* are the ones who created the run on Hector's coin?"

Both Dan and don Fernando nodded yes.

"I knew that there were some whales buying up Hector's coin, but we didn't know who. But Hector and I both watched saw several huge purchases on Coinbase. We thought it was some crypto investment firm or something…”

“Nope,” said Dan. “It was these two brothers. They were pumping up Hector’s coin in order to inflate the value of their futures contracts.”

“Wow!” said Ricardo. “That’s crazy.”

“Anyway, these two brothers are in Panama. In fact, they are in La Chorrera.”

“In La Chorrera?” exclaimed Ricardo. “Why?”

“No one knows,” said Dan. “That’s why the FBI are here. They’ve been tracking these two guys, but they don’t know why they’re here. But you know… used bitcoin is here… Hector is here… and *you* are here.”

It was at this point that even Ricardo’s lawyer brain began to get alarmed. “Do they think *I’m* connected with these two brothers? he blurted out.

“I think that’s why he wants to talk with you,” Dan said. “This FBI guy said that he knew that there was no connection between Hector’s used bitcoin and the scam that these two brothers were running. He said that this was the brothers’ MO—to counterfeit existing cryptocurrency products. And he said he had no evidence that you had ever communicated with these two brothers. But since the brothers were here, and you are here, his theory was that maybe they were here to meet you.”

Now Ricardo’s brain was spinning. “That’s crazy, Dan.”

“It gets worse, Ricardo. He told us that they had been monitoring all your emails, texts, and phone calls. That’s how he knew you had no communication with these two brothers.”

Ricardo’s face went pale for a second, then flushed red. Now he was angry. “Those motherfuckers,” he said. “They’ve been reading my emails and texts!?”

Dan nodded yes.

Ricardo was quiet for a moment while his lawyer brain tried to rein in his panic brain. “Jeez,” he finally said.

"Well, that should prove that I don't know these guys."

"I would think so," agreed Dan. "This FBI guy was clear that he didn't know of any connection between you and these two brothers. But that was the reason he wanted to talk with you."

Ricardo nodded. Finally, he said, "Well, why don't you bring this guy over? I've got nothing to hide."

Don Fernando spoke up. "Oh, one little thing, a minor detail. This FBI agent doesn't know that we know you. And he certainly doesn't know that we are here telling you all this."

"Ahh, yes... I understand," said Ricardo.

And that, dear Reader, is how Dan and don Fernando told Ricardo about Agent Brian Rooney. The three men talked some more and ended up agreeing to bring FBI Agent Brian Rooney over to Dan's apartment later that evening. After Dan and don Fernando left Ricardo's apartment, don Fernando called Agent Rooney and explained in broken English that his network of informants had located Ricardo Mendes, and that it could be arranged that Dan and don Fernando take Agent Rooney over to Ricardo's apartment later that very evening to meet Ricardo. Don Fernando also tried to plant some seeds in Agent Rooney's mind by telling him that his network of informants were convinced that Ricardo Mendes did not know the Lukov brothers, and that he had only been a legal advisor for the used bitcoin project. Of course, don Fernando left out any references to his nephew, Hector Gonzalez.

And speaking of Hector Gonzalez, I should tell you that at the very same moment that don Fernando was talking on the phone with Agent Rooney, Hector was sitting in his living room at his parents' new house in La Chorrera, talking to his parents and trying to explain a problem that he was having with his new project, the Gente Coin.

"I met with Carlos Wang this morning, and we were looking at how my new Gente Coin Project is doing," Hector said. "We have a problem."

His parents nodded attentively. They had never understood his used bitcoin project, and they certainly did not understand this new Gente Coin project. But they did very much appreciate the new house he had bought them, so they were listening carefully.

"Well, the problem is that the Gente Coin subscribers are growing too fast," Hector explained. "It's has become more popular than we anticipated."

"But that is good, isn't it?" his father asked. "That means people are sending you money, right?"

"Oh yes," Hector replied. "The money is flowing into the trust fund that señor Ricardo set up. That's happening automatically. But the problem is one of *capacity*. For every new subscriber to Gente Coin, I have to dedicate a certain amount of space on my server to generate and process and market whatever meme coin the subscriber creates. It's not a lot of space, but we're getting so many subscribers that it adds up."

His parents nodded again, but they looked confused. Hector decided to simplify his explanation. "Remember when cousin Rafael was driving for Uber in Panama City, and he liked picking up people at the airport because they always tipped him well? But then he had to buy a bigger car, because his customers had so much luggage? That's like my problem. I need more computing power to service all the new customers I'm getting."

"You already have three computers in your room," his father said. "Do you think you need to buy a fourth one?"

"No, no, no," said Hector. "I don't run the Gente Coin program on my computers here at home. I have to rent servers in Panama City. It's a big program, and it needs a lot of computing power."

His parents looked at each other. "What exactly is a server, Hector?" his father asked.

"It's a very very big computer, dad. I rent space on several servers at Serverlocity in Panama City. The Gente

Coin project handles huge amounts of data. Anyway, Carlos Wang and I figured out today that we need to rent more servers. I talked with the people at Serverlocity and they have the equipment. But it's going to cost me several thousand dollars a month to rent new servers. But Carlos and I realized today that we need to move fast on this. Our subscriber base is growing so rapidly, that we estimate we only have a week before we will not be able to handle any new subscribers."

"Ah, I understand," his father said. "You need to tap into the trust fund to rent these server things in Panama City."

"Exactly," said Hector.

"And you need our permission to access trust fund money."

"Exactly."

"And by renting more server things, this new project will grow and make even more money."

"Exactly."

"Then you have our permission, Hector. But I think you also need to go and explain this to señor Ricardo."

"Yes, of course, dad. I was thinking of going over to his apartment tonight and telling him. As I said, we have to get the new servers online this week to handle all of our new clients."

And that, dear Reader, is how Hector Gonzalez ended up going over to Ricardo's apartment that very night. I told you it was going to be a perfect storm. Fate may or may not be a series of random events in a chaotic and meaningless universe, but every once in a while, the tumblers of random events line up just perfectly. And thus it was that on *this particular night*, Ricardo was opening the door to let Hector enter his apartment; just as very drunk Jerry Armen was pointing to Ricardo's apartment from the street as he and the Lukov brothers were climbing out of their cab; just at the exact same moment that Izzy parked his car discretely away from the Lukov brothers' cab that he had been following; just as Dan and don Fernando and FBI Agent Rooney were driving into Ricardo's neighborhood.

CHAPTER SIXTEEN

Ricardo heard a knock on his door. He was expecting it to be Dan and don Fernando bringing over this FBI agent to talk to him—because, you remember, that was the plan—but when he asked who it was, he was surprised to hear Hector's voice. He opened the door and there was Hector Gonzalez standing there, smiling.

Now, let me say again, dear Reader, that what happened that night in Ricardo's apartment was a perfect storm. And perfect storms can move extremely fast. The events that lead up to them are often slow and always unnoticed, like water receding from a beach, but then, the tsunami hits, and the next thing you know, you are downing under hundreds of feet of water. So, understand that what happened in Ricardo's apartment that night only took maybe five minutes—everything happened *that* fast—but I'm going to have to explain it bit by bit. So bear with me.

"Hector! Hey, how are you? Come on in," Ricardo exclaimed.

"I am sorry to intrude, don Ricardo, but I have something to ask you. This will only take a second."

"No worries. Come in, come in. What's up?"

"Well, I've been working with Carlos Wang, you know, with this launch of the Gente Coin project, and the orders are coming in."

"Ah, that's good, Hector."

"Yes. Well, it is too good, you see, because the orders are coming in too fast. And Carlos and I are going to run out of server space soon. We're going to need to rent another server, maybe two more, from Serverlocity in Panama City."

So, dear Reader, while Hector was explaining to Ricardo why he needed the trust fund to release more money to allow him to rent more server space, the drunken Jerry Armen was leading the Lukov brothers up the stairs towards Ricardo's apartment, and he was whispering to them all the way up.

"You have to understand, my friends, that this Ricardo is an evil, evil man," Jerry was saying in a hushed but emphatic tone. "He is the mastermind behind the used bitcoin, and he owes me a million dollars!"

Now the Lukov brothers didn't give two shits whether Ricardo owed Jerry any money. In fact, during the taxi ride over to Ricardo's apartment, the Lukov brothers had both independently decided that they very much did not like this Jerry Armen person. For the entire taxi ride, he was spewing forth a drunken story about how much he hated Ricardo. And understand, the Lukov brothers did not hate Ricardo. In fact, they admired him. They did not know whether he was the mastermind behind used bitcoin or not, but they knew he had played a pivotal role in creating the used bitcoin account on Coinbase; and they knew that used bitcoin had gotten famous in the cryptocurrency world; and they knew that their own used bitcoin futures scam had made them millions of dollars. So, they had a very favorable attitude towards Ricardo. Ricardo was the reason they had traveled all the way from Switzerland to Panama. They wanted to meet him. They wanted to be friends with him. They wanted to somehow convince him to join forces and make even more money. Jerry Armen was simply the means whereby they could meet Ricardo. Jerry Armen was a disposable stooge in the Lukov brothers' mind. And in the cab ride over to Ricardo's apartment, each of the Lukov brothers had independently decided that they needed to be rid of Jerry Armen as soon as they met Ricardo. A drunken hateful loudmouth Jerry Armen would be of no use to their plans after they were introduced to Ricardo. So, in the cab ride over to Ricardo's apartment, the two Lukov brothers had given each other a knowing look while Jerry was ranting on about how evil Ricardo was. Being twins, the Lukov brothers were almost psychic. They knew what each other was thinking. And they were both thinking that Jerry needed to be disposed of quickly.

So, as Jerry was leading them up the stairs to Ricardo's apartment and whispering about Ricardo, each of the Lukov brothers were considering various ways in which they could be rid of this drunken American once they met Ricardo.

Near the bottom of the stairwell, in the shadows, Izzy was watching Jerry lead the Lukov brothers up the stairs. He didn't know the Lukov brothers; he didn't know whose apartment they were going to; he only knew that his target was Jerry. Enforcers such as Izzy are rather primitive creatures. They operate in a very basic manner, much like a crocodile or a shark. Izzy had been sent by his bosses to simply convey a message to Jerry. Conveying that message was the only agenda that Izzy had. His job was to convince Jerry that if he did not pay the million dollars he owed, that he would die a horrible painful death. Izzy's usual method of conveying such a method was to administer a painful beating and then later verbally explain to his victim why he had been beaten and why he would be beaten again unless he paid. But now, Izzy had a problem, and his problem was the two men that were following Jerry up the apartment stairs. Witnesses were never included in any of Izzy's plans. But Izzy decided that maybe he could use these two men to convey his message to Jerry. If he were to shoot the two men in front of Jerry, Izzy thought, that would serve to convince Jerry that Izzy's bosses were serious about getting the money that was owed him. Yes, Izzy thought, that was a good plan. He would simply murder the two men in front of Jerry. That would make it so much simpler to speak to Jerry. He would only need to use one sentence. He could simply say that if Jerry didn't pay his debt, that he would be next. It would be a direct and convincing conversation. Plus, he wouldn't need to explain anything. Izzy liked that. He was a man of few words.

And so it was that Izzy waited at the bottom of the stairwell until Jerry and the Lukov brothers got to the top of the landing and turned to walk down the balcony to Ricardo's apartment. As soon as those three men turned to where they couldn't see the stairwell, Izzy quickly and silently crept up the stairs.

And at that exact same moment, Dan and don Fernando and FBI agent Brian Rooney were getting out of don Fernando's car and heading towards the stairwell. The ride over to Ricardo's apartment had been quiet. Neither Dan nor don Fernando wanted to say anything that would tip Agent Rooney off to the fact that they knew Ricardo. But they had to be careful not to lie and directly say that they didn't know him. When it comes to plausible deniability, the key is *not talking much*. Luckily, Agent Rooney was reviewing his file on Ricardo and didn't notice that the two men were being quiet.

As it happened, don Fernando parked right behind Izzy's car. They arrived just as Izzy was standing at the bottom of the stairwell watching Jerry and the Lukov brothers disappear at the top of the landing. Izzy didn't see or hear don Fernando's car; and don Fernando and Dan didn't see Izzy start to climb the stairs.

"This way," Dan said as he led Agent Rooney toward the stairwell that led to Ricardo's second floor apartment. Don Fernando followed silently.

And thus it was, dear Reader, that all the dark clouds had gathered in the sky, and the heavens were about to break open and unleash the perfect storm directly to the inside of Ricardo's apartment.

For as Hector was explaining to Ricardo why he needed the trust fund to release a new payment to the Serverlocity company in Panama City, Jerry knocked loudly on Ricardo's door. Ricardo assumed that this was his expected guests of don Fernando and Dan bringing the FBI agent over to talk with him, so he opened the door, this time without asking who was there. And for the second time that night, he was surprised to see someone he didn't expect in his doorway. It was Jerry and two large men who Ricardo didn't recognize. Ricardo recognized Jerry, of course. He had seen him at his door before, and more recently, at the hospital. Ricardo's adrenaline suddenly began to surge. Hector, of course, did not know what was happening. He simply heard a knock on the door, and saw Ricardo open the door, and then heard a strange man shout, "That's him!" But Hector's adrenaline also started to pump, because he sensed that something bad was going to happen, but his adrenaline made him freeze, like a deer in the headlights, unable to move.

It was at this point, dear Reader, that the perfect storm hit. At that exact moment, the dimension of time both sped up and slowed down simultaneously. The events that I'm going to describe to you happened in less than thirty seconds. But from Hector's viewpoint, it all played out in very slow motion.

"That's him!" Jerry shouted and pointed to Ricardo. At this point, Jerry stepped boldly into Ricardo's apartment followed by the Lukov brothers. In Jerry's drunken mind, he had assumed that Ricardo was going to think that the Lukov brothers were Jerry's musclemen. Jerry planned to threaten Ricardo with his knife and demand that Ricardo pay him one million dollars. Jerry was operating under the delusion that the Lukov brothers were going to quietly and menacingly stand behind him. So, Jerry was shocked when Georgi Lukov stepped in front of him and said to Ricardo, "Mr. Mendes, we are big fans of yours and have traveled all the way from Switzerland to meet you."

Jerry panicked. This was not the way that things were supposed to go down. The Lukov brothers were supposed to simply stand silently behind him while he demanded that Ricardo give him back the million dollars that he had lost on Laissez trading platform. But now, one of these two guys was greeting Ricardo like an old friend! Something was wrong!

He had to do something! So, he reached for the hunting knife that was in the sheath on his belt.

At the exact moment that Izzy reached the second-floor landing, he heard Jerry shout, "That's him," and his adrenaline also kicked in. For a creature like Izzy, adrenaline has the opposite effect that it had on Hector. Hector was frozen in place, like an ice statue, watching as events unfolded around him. But adrenaline in Izzy gave him action, pure action. He bolted to the door with not a single thought in his head, except to move through time and space and take action.

Dan and don Fernando and Agent Rooney were at the foot of the stairwell when they also heard Jerry shout, "That's him!" Don Fernando and Agent Rooney, being police officers, were very familiar with the tonal differences between a menacing shout and a friendly shout. Dan, being a retired detective, also recognized that Jerry's shout was a cry to arms, a threatening banner of sound meant to signal danger. So, all three men instinctively began to sprint up the stairway to the second floor.

And thus it was, dear Reader, that the perfect storm exploded. Georgi Lukov was just about to start his second sentence to Ricardo. He was going to introduce himself and his brother. Dimitar Lukov had already reached his hand up and placed it on Jerry's shoulder. The two Lukov brothers had telepathically decided that Dimitar would block any further interference from Jerry while Georgi did the talking.

Jerry felt Dimitar's hand on his shoulder applying a restraining pressure, just as Jerry's hand reached the handle of his hunting knife. He pulled the large knife out in one sweeping motion and held it high. Everyone in the room saw the light shimmer and reflect off the silver metal. Jerry shouted, "No!" and stepped in front of Georgi, moving toward Ricardo, waving the knife back and forth in front of him in a slicing motion.

Georgi turned halfway toward Jerry and reached for the gun at his hip. His brother Dimitar simultaneously reached for his gun. They couldn't let this demented American fuck up their plans. They needed Ricardo alive.

Dan, don Fernando, and Agent Rooney burst into the room. All three men saw Jerry waving the knife. Don Fernando and Agent Rooney reached for their guns. Agent Rooney shouted, "Everybody freeze!" as loud as he could.

However, the words "Everybody freeze" had just the opposite effect: everyone jumped. There were too many people crowded at the door, and a man was waving a knife. So everyone instinctively jumped back and spread themselves apart and looked at both the knife and at the men who had just entered the apartment.

And in that split second, the entire world seemed to stop and be frozen in space. In those dangerous moments when time stops, the brain goes into hyper-drive. Agent Rooney recognized the Lukov brothers from the photographs in his file. He could only see the back of Jerry's head, so he didn't know who he was. But he could see the other man in front of Jerry, and Agent Rooney assumed that that man was Ricardo. He had no idea who the teenager was frozen in fear next to Ricardo. And he had no idea who the other large man was standing behind the Lukov brothers, but that man seemed to be reaching for something which Agent Rooney assumed would be a gun.

It was the Lukov brothers who fired first. It was a simultaneous act, the way that twins do. They both pulled their guns and shot Jerry. They each fired without hesitation because they both knew that legally they were protected. This drunk was trying to kill their future business partner. It was a case of pure self-defense of others. The fact that they were shooting Jerry in the back was irrelevant. Jerry's body jerked forward from the impact of the bullets and fell at Ricardo's feet. Hector's eyes bulged, and his bladder emptied as he peed in his pants.

Just as the Lukov brothers' shots filled the air, Izzy's hand reached his gun. He didn't know who these two thugs were, but they had just killed a million-dollar client. He didn't care for Jerry, but keeping Jerry alive to pay back his debt was Izzy's job. Izzy pulled his gun out and fired at the Lukov brothers.

But there were two Lukov brothers, each with guns in their hands, and Izzy didn't know which one to shoot first, so he just fired. But he missed. His bullet passed in between both men, went through the room, and grazed Hector's arm. Hector felt the pain and spun around to his left, falling towards the floor.

Agent Rooney's highly trained brain was making a million calculations at once. He had seen the Lukov brothers shoot the man with a knife, but he recognized that the man with the knife was attacking the man whom he assumed was Ricardo. And the Lukov brothers had only shot once and then stopped. But now this other unknown man had shot and hit that boy. Clearly the other man was the biggest threat. So, Agent Rooney aimed and shot Izzy.

Izzy had been standing in such a way that Agent Rooney had to shoot between the Lukov brothers to hit him. But Agent Rooney was a trained marksman, and he hit Izzy straight in the heart. Izzy's body flew back against the wall, and he and his gun fell to the floor.

But the Lukov brothers, who had turned to face Agent Rooney, didn't see Izzy get hit behind them. They only saw Agent Rooney shooting towards *them*, so they immediately opened fire on Agent Rooney. The Lukov brothers were not great shots, but there were two of them, and their bullets hit Agent Rooney before Agent Rooney could shoot again. Agent Rooney slumped to the ground.

By this time, don Fernando had pulled out his gun, aimed it at the Lukov brothers and shouted, "Police! Stop!" in his booming loud voice.

Now, I should remind you that don Fernando had been the chief of police for almost thirty years, and there was something about him, something about his presence, his look, his voice, that simply commanded respect. He embodied police authority in every aspect of his being. And so, when the Lukov brothers heard him shout "Police! Stop!" they stopped and put their hands up.

Don Fernando reached into the breast pocket of his jacket and pulled out his badge and identification. "I am Police Chief José Fernando. Place both of your weapons on the ground slowly."

The Lukov brothers did as they were told. In each of their minds, they were calculating the situation. They had shot Jerry because he was attacking Ricardo, and they had shot this other man because he was shooting at them. This police chief was a witness to all of this. They couldn't be changed with any crime. They were innocent. Of course, there would be an inquiry and bureaucracy, but they would be exonerated. Somehow, both Lukov brothers made the exact same calculations. They glanced at each other and nodded in reassurance.

Dan and don Fernando both stepped over to the Lukov brothers. Don Fernando used his only pair of handcuffs to secure Georgi Lukov's hands behind his back. Dan used his belt to tie Dimitar's hands behind his back. Don Fernando patted both men down for any other weapons and then told them to sit on the couch.

"We didn't do anything wrong!" Georgi said. "That man with the knife was attacking Ricardo Mendes, and the other man was trying to kill us!"

Don Fernando intuited what he needed to say. "We just need to sort this thing out." That seemed to calm the two brothers, as they sat down on the couch.

Ricardo was checking on Hector. Hector's arm was bleeding, but not badly. Ricardo helped him up from the floor and sat him in a chair. He grabbed some paper towels from the kitchen and told Hector to press them tightly against the wound. He reassured Hector that it was not bad, and that he was going to be okay.

Dan used his cell phone to call for ambulances. Don Fernando was on his cell phone, calling for police backup. Dan checked on Agent Rooney. He was dead. Dan also checked on Izzy and Jerry. Both also dead.

A minute later, Ricardo's tiny apartment was filled with police officers. Several ambulances arrived quickly. Don Fernando directed them to take Hector to the hospital first. The three bodies on the floor had to go to the hospital too, to be officially pronounced dead. But there was no hurry about that. Dead is dead.

One of the police officers put cuffs on Dimitar and gave Dan back his belt. Every time that the Lukov brothers tried to say something, don Fernando repeated what he said earlier. "We just need to sort things out." But secretly, don Fernando knew there was nothing to sort out. These two men had killed an FBI agent. No matter what Panamanian law said, US law would put these two in jail for the rest of their lives.

The police took the Lukov brothers down to the station to be processed and put into a holding cell. Don Fernando told one of the police sergeants to call the US authorities and let them know that one of their agents had been murdered. An official police photographer took photos of Ricardo's living room. Another police officer took a statement from Ricardo.

At one point, Dan turned to don Fernando. "What the fuck was that all about?"

"I don't know, Dani," don Fernando replied. "We will just have to piece it all together when we learn who these men are... or I should say, who they were."

And that, dear Reader, is how all perfect storms end. You are left, standing in the middle of the wreckage, trying to put the pieces back together, trying to figure out just what the fuck had happened.

CHAPTER SEVENTEEN

And so, to recap, dear Reader: Agent Brian Rooney was dead. Don Fernando had been right about the rage of the FBI having one of its men killed in the line of official duty. Nothing that the Lukov brothers could say stopped the FBI from immediately flying down to Panama and extraditing the two brothers back to the United States to face capital murder charges. For good measure, the FBI also slapped about thirty money laundering and cryptocurrency fraud charges on the pile. The Lukov brothers were toast.

Izzy was dead. No one was able to really connect the dots on him. It was only when don Fernando pushed Izzy's body over on the floor of Ricardo's apartment, that don Fernando recognized him as the same man he had seen in the surveillance video walking through the lobby of the hotel to beat up Jerry. Don Fernando knew his real name, of course. And he remembered that Izzy had been on an FBI watchlist of possible mafia-connected persons. But that was really all that he or anyone else knew. No one ever figured out that this dead man was working for Izzy Brothers Capital, which was controlled by the Genovese crime family, and that Izzy Brothers Capital had bought Jerry's gambling debt from the brokerage firm of Pollock and Malpeso, who had bought the debt from the Laissez cryptocurrency trading platform. So, no one could connect Izzy with Jerry Armen, because no one realized that Jerry had incurred a million-dollar debt making leveraged bets on used bitcoins on the Laissez platform. But what don Fernando did know was that Izzy had some beef with Jerry, and that he had beaten Jerry up and had broken Jerry's arm, and so don Fernando correctly assumed that Izzy had followed Jerry to Ricardo's apartment that night.

And, of course, Jerry was dead. Dan did some internet sleuthing for don Fernando and found out that Jerry was a social media crypto-influencer, and that he had been posting false and hateful claims against used bitcoins. And don Fernando interviewed the bartender at Jerry's hotel, who described how the drunken Jerry had gotten friendly with the Lukov brothers in the bar that night, and how they had all left together. There didn't seem to be any connection between the Lukov brothers and Ricardo, so don Fernando could only assume that Jerry had taken the Lukov brothers over to Ricardo's apartment. This seemed to fit with the interview that don Fernando had with the cab driver who picked up Jerry and the Lukov brothers at the hotel bar that night. The cab driver described how it was Jerry who was giving directions about how to get to Ricardo's apartment in Villa Rosario.

The only thing that connected Jerry and the Lukov brothers with Ricardo was that they all were associated in some way with used bitcoin. But no one knew the whole story.

Ricardo was left quite traumatized by the whole event. One moment he was having a pleasant conversation with Hector in his apartment, and the next moment, there was the deafening explosion of gunfire, filling the air with an acrid smell of gunpowder and leaving three dead men on his floor. He had to have a cleaning crew come in the next day to clean up every molecule of blood that was splattered on his floor and walls. Even after a week, his hands couldn't stop shaking. He had trouble sleeping. He couldn't walk into his living room without anxiety. His doctor gave him some anxiety pills, and that helped to calm him down.

Hector was also traumatized by what he had witnessed. The ambulance had taken him to the emergency room, and the doctors there had treated his arm. Luckily, the bullet had only grazed him. The doctors bandaged him up and sent him home. They told him he would probably have a scar on his arm for the rest of his life. They did not tell him about the emotional scar. You see, dear Reader, actually witnessing murder is quite different than watching one in a video game. Hector, like all teenagers—and like most adults—thought he was mature. He had seen plenty of murders on TV, in video games, and in movies. He thought he knew what death was. But seeing someone get shot and bleed out and die right in front of you is something very, very different. The human brain is not prepared for that, not prepared for seeing the agony of death on another human being's face, not prepared for the gargling sound of a person's last breath as they drown in their own blood, not prepared for the bright red color of blood as it gushes unstoppably out of a chest wound. Those images would stay with Hector his whole life.

Don Fernando went to visit Hector the next day for two reasons. As Hector's uncle, he wanted to see how his nephew was doing. But as a police officer, he needed to fill in some of the missing pieces in his understanding of what had happened. Ricardo had already explained to don Fernando that Hector had simply dropped by his apartment to update him on how the new Gente Coin project was going. So, don Fernando was convinced that Hector's presence was purely coincidental. But he was curious as to whether Hector had ever been contacted by Jerry or Izzy or the Lukov brothers before that night. In don Fernando's mind, it was still unexplainable how events had conspired to place so many people in Ricardo's tiny apartment, all at the exact same time the night before. There *had* to be some logical reason for it. But of course, logic had nothing to do with it. Logic, dear Reader, never has anything to do with Fate.

But we humans are burdened with the need to make sense out of things. And so it was that don Fernando was gently questioning Hector that next day.

"So, how is the arm, Hector?" don Fernando asked.

"It hurts a little, uncle, but I can move it fine. The doctor said I was going to be alright. He said I can take the bandage off in two days, and he gave me some ointment to put on the wound."

"Ah, Hector, I am glad to hear this. I was worried. I did call the doctor before I came over, and he told me that the bullet just broke the skin. You are very lucky."

"I don't *feel* lucky, uncle. It was a terrible experience. I was real scared."

"Yes, I understand, Hector, I understand. Tell me, these strange men who came over to Ricardo's apartment last night—did you know any of them?"

"No, uncle. I mean, I know señor Landes, but he was the only one."

Don Fernando reached into his pocket and pulled out a piece of paper and handed it to Hector.

"These are the names of all those people. Did any of them ever email you or try to contact you?"

Hector read the names on the paper and shook his head. "No, uncle. I have never seen these names before."

"Hmm," said don Fernando. "Neither has Ricardo. They were strangers to him, too."

"Who were they, uncle?"

"Well, it is a long story, Hector. The man who came with Dani and me, he was an FBI agent. He was after those two twins. Those twins—the ones we arrested—they were from Russia. It turns out that they had created a scam on the black web, a scam that pretended to sell futures of *your* used bitcoin. Evidently, a lot of people lost money to these two twins. So, the FBI was after them. This FBI agent had followed them all the way to La Chorrera. But we don't know why they came to Panama. We think it had to have something to do with your coin. But we just don't know. I tried to question those men this morning, but they were closed up tighter than two clams. The FBI is on their way to take them back to the United States. They will be charged with killing the FBI agent and with killing the man with the knife. We really don't know who the man with the knife was. Dani is doing some research on him. He had come to Ricardo's apartment before, but Ricardo wouldn't let him in. He was mad at Ricardo for some reason, but we don't know why. I think he was just a crazy drunk. The other man who died, the one that the FBI agent shot—well, we don't know much about him either, except that he had beaten up the man with knife a few days earlier. The whole situation is, well, to be blunt, it is what the gringos call a cluster-fuck. And we don't know why any of it happened."

Hector nodded. His teenage brain was trying to understand everything, trying to organize the facts into an explanation that fit what he knew of the world. "So... the two twins were bad men, uncle? They were fraudsters from Russia?"

"Yes," said don Fernando. "They were bad men."

"And the man with the knife, was he a bad man, too?"

"Well... yes, I think you could say that, Hector. He was a drunk, and that's bad. And he had a knife and was trying to attack Ricardo. So, yes, I would say he was a bad man."

"So, the two bad Russians shot the bad man with a knife?"

"Yes. I know that seems odd. But sometimes bad men kill each other."

"And the other man," Hector said, "the one who the FBI man killed... he was a bad man, too?"

"Yes," said don Fernando. "We know he worked with the mafia in the United States, so yes, he too was a bad man."

"But then the two Russian twins killed the FBI man, and he was a good man," said Hector.

"Yes," said don Fernando. "The FBI man was a good man."

Hector nodded. It seemed to make it simpler to say out loud who was bad and who was good. "It's a terrible thing when good people die," he said.

"Yes, Hector. It is terrible. It's terrible when anyone dies."

"Why do people kill each other, uncle?"

Don Fernando shook his head back and forth. "I have been police chief for almost thirty years, Hector. And I still don't know the answer to that. I think it has something to do with greed. They each wanted something they didn't have."

Hector thought for a moment. His eyes seemed to tear up.

"Did it all have something to do with me, uncle? Am I somehow... *responsible* for what happened?"

Don Fernando looked surprised. "Of course not, Hector! You are only responsible for yourself. You cannot be responsible for what other people do."

"But I created used bitcoin, uncle. And you say these two Russians used that to scam people. And then they come to Ricardo's apartment with guns!"

"Hector," don Fernando said firmly, "let me tell you clearly. In this life, you are only responsible for yourself. You cannot control what other people do, especially other idiot people. The world is *full* of idiots. And one thing idiots always do, is they try and make you responsible for their bad behaviors. Don't fall for that. You did nothing wrong. You made a funny coin, and people gave you money for it, and you were able to buy your parents a nice house. There's nothing wrong with that. What strangers think or do is not your responsibility."

"But I feel bad, uncle. I *feel* like it's my responsibility."

"That is the human condition, Hector—to feel responsible. But let me ask you this: can you change any of these people or their situations? Can you un-arrest the two Russians? Can you stop a drunk from drinking? Can you stop people from being greedy? If you have no control over others, then you are not responsible for them."

Don Fernando paused, then said. "You are a good boy, Hector. Take care of your parents, finish school. That's all that matters."

Hector nodded. He wasn't convinced, but he said, "Yes, uncle."

CHAPTER EIGHTEEN

Several weeks passed. Hector's arm healed up, leaving only a reddish scar. His doctor told him that that the scar would become less visible with time. Ricardo signed the necessary papers to release money from Hector's trust fund so that he could rent more server space. Hector's Gente Coin project continued to gain subscribers. People all over the world were minting their very own meme coins and placing them on Coinbase to trade or sell. In fact, Hector and Carlos Wang were amazed to watch their subscriber base grow to almost six million people. Hector couldn't believe that so many people were sending him money just so they could create a meme coin that had absolutely no value. Carlos did some sampling of the types of coins that people were creating. Almost all of them bore the image of the face of their creators, like old Roman coins stamped with reliefs of dead emperors' faces. Carlos joked with Hector that God created man in His own image, and so naturally men would create meme coins in their own image.

A larger apartment opened up in Ricardo's apartment building, several doors down from Ricardo's apartment. Not only was it more spacious, but it had a better view from the balcony. So it was a no-brainer that Ricardo took it. The lease was a bit more expensive, of course, but Ricardo was glad to move out of his old apartment. He just couldn't shake the feeling of dread that living there brought him.

Dan kept digging into Jerry's social media footprint. He ended up interviewing several other crypto-currency vloggers in the US, including Gloria María Hernández and Roger Van Kette, and they all told him the rumor that they had heard that Jerry had lost a million dollars gambling on used bitcoin derivatives on the Laissez crypt-currency platform. That made sense to Dan. It seemed to explain Jerry's vendetta against used bitcoin. Maybe, somehow, Dan thought, Jerry had associated Ricardo with used bitcoin, and was seeking revenge.

The Lukov brothers languished in a US federal prison, awaiting trial for the murders of FBI agent Brian Rooney and Jerry Armen. The US government tried to freeze what assets of the two brothers that they could reach, but Switzerland and Bulgaria blocked the US government from seizing the tens of millions of dollars that the Lukov brothers had stashed away in those two countries. But that still left the Lukov brothers unable to raise any money to hire a private lawyer. The court, of course, appointed an overworked public defender to represent them. But the Lukov brothers really needed an army of lawyers to fight the mountain of charges they were facing. As I said earlier, they were toast.

The body of FBI agent Rooney was given a hero's burial. The FBI lauded him for cracking the case of the Lukov brothers and protecting thousands of Americans from being defrauded. Of course, he had done no such thing. He had merely shot Izzy that night in Ricardo's apartment out of pure reflex, because Izzy had shot Jerry. In private conversations, FBI officials acknowledged to each other that agent Rooney was no hero, and that, in fact, he had fucked up and gotten himself killed. But that story didn't improve the image of the FBI, So publicly, they proclaimed him a hero.

The Panamanian government kept Izzy's body on ice in the morgue several weeks, but no one claimed his body. He was eventually buried in a pauper's grave outside of Panama City. He didn't even receive a headstone with his real name. His employer, Izzy Brothers Capital, wrote off most of Jerry's debt that they had bought from the brokerage firm of Pollock and Malpeso. They shouldn't have been allowed to write it off, because they had bought the debt for pennies on the dollar. But in fact, Izzy Brothers Capital managed to come out ahead on the deal. With tax loopholes being what they are, writing off the million-dollar debt netted Izzy

Brothers Capital even more money. So they were satisfied with the outcome.

Some distant relative of Jerry's—an aunt in Philadelphia—paid for Jerry's body to be cremated in Panama, and for the ashes to be shipped back to the United States. His YouTube Channel went silent. The other vloggers, podcasters and cryptocurrency influencers never mentioned him again. He was yesterday's news. His old podcasts still existed on the internet, of course, but no one ever fished them out to view them, and Jerry Armen was soon forgotten.

The memory of used bitcoin faded from public consciousness as well, along with the millions of dog coins, cat coins, monkey coins, and other fads, trends, whims, and crazes of history. The public's short-term memory is no better than the average Alzheimer's patient. When it comes to the folly of any type of speculation, out of sight is always out of mind.

Hector, on the other hand, had not forgotten about used bitcoin. How could he? Every day he woke up in the comfortable house that he had bought for his parents. Every day he went to a nice school that was so much better than his old high school back in Villa Rosario. All due to used bitcoin. But his mind was divided, conflicted. On one hand, he thanked God every day that he had invented used bitcoin and Gente Coin. Every morning, he climbed out of his soft bed and went to his new computer, logged into his administrator account at his Worthless Cryptocurrency website and checked how many new Gente Coin subscribers he had gained overnight. Every new subscriber was another one hundred dollars pure profit into his pocket, and every morning he was amazed to see thousands of new subscribers.

But on the other hand, he was still plagued by what had happened that night weeks ago in Ricardo's apartment. He couldn't stop thinking about what it all meant. The more he thought about it, and the more he tried to understand his connection to those events, the more tormented and divided his mind became. He simply couldn't enjoy all his new surroundings without feeling guilty. Maybe, dear Reader, guilty is the wrong word. Hector thought about what his uncle had told him in the hospital, about how he wasn't responsible for what stupid people did. He thought hard about that. Finally, he decided that what he was feeling wasn't guilt. Finally, he decided that the awful feeling that he had was a feeling of *complicity*. And finally, when he couldn't stand it anymore, he called Ricardo and asked if he could come over to talk.

"Hector, come in, come in," Ricardo said when he opened the door. "Welcome to my new apartment. Isn't it grand?"

Hector looked around. "It is very nice, don Ricardo. You have much more space here."

"Yes, and I bought new furniture, see? A bigger writing table, and a new sofa. Try it out."

Hector sat down on the large sofa. "This is very comfortable, don Ricardo, very nice."

"Yes, well, I needed a change, Hector. I really wanted to move out of my old apartment. I was lucky that this one became available. I think I can stay here for many years."

"Yes, it is very nice, don Ricardo."

"Now, tell me Hector, what can I do for you? You said you wanted to talk."

Hector pursed his lips and nodded slowly. "Don Ricardo, I know the Gente Coin project is doing well. It's doing very well. But I want... I want to get out of it. I remember you told me once about crypto hedge funds that buy cryptocurrency projects. I would like to ask you to find one of those hedge funds for me and sell them my Gente Coin business."

"Say more, Hector," said Ricardo. "Why do you want to sell it?"

"It is hard to explain, don Ricardo. But my new school requires more history classes than my old school did in Villa Rosario, and I am learning things I never knew about before.

Right now, we are studying the Second World War, and I was reading all about how the German Nazis occupied France. And I was reading about how the French government, after the Nazis invaded France, how they collaborated with the Nazis and helped them deport Jews. And my teacher explained that the French government did this because France was in desperate economic times, and the Nazis had more guns, and so it was a pragmatic decision by the government to collaborate. But it made me very sad, don Ricardo. And I thought the French government should have resisted. They didn't have to collaborate. And it made me think about my situation. My family was very poor in Villa Rosario, remember? Every rainy season, our roof leaked, and we had to move the beds so we wouldn't get wet at night. I was desperate to make money. I thought that used bitcoin would be the way to help my family. So, I worked hard on it, to make it work. And it did work, but it brought all those bad people to my town. My uncle says that I'm not responsible for what happened. He says that stupid people make bad decisions all the time. But I can't help but feel that if it wasn't for used bitcoin, none of those bad things would have happened. Those Russians would not have invented used bitcoin *futures* and ripped off innocent people, and they would not have come to your apartment and killed people..."

Ricardo nodded, then said, "But those two Russians would have just invented some other scam, Hector. They would have still ripped people off."

"Yes," replied Hector, "but *I* wouldn't have been involved. *I* wouldn't have been a part of it... Anyway, I have decided that I don't want to be a part of it anymore. I don't want anything to do with cryptocurrency. It's all just a big scam, and I don't want to profit off it anymore... I realized, don Ricardo, that I was lucky. I was just amazingly lucky. So many people have lost all their money on cryptocurrency. I want to quit now, while I'm ahead. I have enough—more than enough—money for me and my family. It's enough! I talked to my parents about this, and they understand. So... can you help me get rid of Gente Coin?"

Ricardo nodded again. "Of course, Hector, of course. In fact, now is probably a good time to sell, while Gente Coin is hot. You want to sell the whole thing—all of it?

Hector nodded. "I want out completely, don Ricardo. I never want anything to do with the crypto world again."

"Okay, Hector, we can do that. Have you thought about what price you want to ask for the Gente Coin business?"

"No, don Ricardo, can I leave that up to you?"

"I tell you what, Hector," Ricardo said. "Let me send out some query emails. There are many crypto hedge funds now, and they seem to be flush with money. Why don't you come back in about an hour, and we'll see what kind of response we get. We can set a price depending on how many replies we receive. The more replies, the higher the price."

"I want to sell it fast, don Ricardo."

"I understand, Hector. Come back in an hour, and we'll talk some more."

And that, dear Reader, is how Hector got out of the cryptocurrency business. There are at least thirty mega-billionaire venture capital firms and hedge funds that specialize in blockchain technology and cryptocurrency projects. They all love to buy up and exploit start-up crypto-ventures like Gente Coin. And so it was that Ricardo had no problem arranging the sale of Hector's Gente Coin business. The final sale price was beyond Hector's—and even Ricardo's—wildest dreams. Let's just say that Hector was not only the richest *teenager* in the province of West Panama; he was the richest *person* in that whole province. There were many adaptations that he and his family had to make. They had to move again, this time to a gated high-security condominium. They had to buy a bullet-proof car and hire a driver, because, after all, they still lived in Panama. They also had to hire a bodyguard to escort Hector back and forth to school. Hector had to get off social media entirely. Being rich means you are no longer anonymous. And when you are no longer anonymous, you lose many of your freedoms. Hector could no longer simply go where he wanted on a whim. He had to plan his activities. Still, in general, Hector was happy. His conscience was clean, and that was the important thing. He slept well at night. He was free of the seductions, the addiction and, dare I say, the complete delusion of cryptocurrency. People talk about surfing the web... well, Hector had caught the perfect wave in very polluted water and had ridden it all the way to the shore.

And thus, our little story comes to an end. And what have we learned, dear Reader? Maybe nothing. Hector slept well at night, but so did Ricardo, and Dan, and don Fernando. Maybe the secret of life is just dodging bullets. Maybe life is rich in terms of the things you can afford to leave alone.

Maybe happiness lies in knowing when you have enough.

I don't know. I'm not a philosopher. I just tell stories.

-fin-

ABOUT THE AUTHOR

Robert Rahula was born in Spain to an American father and Spanish mother but grew up in Virginia on the farm of his paternal grandparents. He returned to Menorca, Spain in the 1960s to pursue his writing career. Over the past thirty years, Robert has published dozens of books of prose and poetry in Spain and in the United States. Readings of his poems appear on his YouTube channel, his Facebook page, and his website robertrahula.com. He travels Europe and Central and South America for several months a year, giving readings and lectures, and spends the rest of his time writing.

www.ingramcontent.com/pod-product-compliance
Lightning Source LLC
Chambersburg PA
CBHW071334150726
47997CB00002B/721